The Beta's Mate

Blue Moon Book 2

Alexa Phoenix

Copyright © 2022 Alexa Phoenix

All rights reserved.

ISBN: 9798415365074

DEDICATION

For the protective men who treat their women like queens and have the massive dick to back it all up. We fantasize about you.

From author Alexa Phoenix, comes a steamy, paranormal romance.

Alexi

Meeting your soulmate is one of the most exciting and important parts of being a wolf. But it seems that mine is intent on running. So now I find myself in a constant game of chase to try and work out why.

Verity

Throughout my life I have always been told that I'm the runt of the litter and undeserving of what normal wolves have. But one day that was set to change, I met him.. Alexi.
From the moment I met him I felt a sudden change. How can one person spark such a feeling?
But as I try to focus on my future I am inundated with the abuse from my past.
I just hope that one day I can finally be happy.

Alexa Phoenix

Chapter 1

Andy's POV

So, my life somehow got so much better...

The worst experience in my life was when my mate rejected me when I turned 18, but that led me to Logan, the sweetest man I've ever met. It was as if the Goddess apologised for making me deal with Connor by making Logan my second chance mate!

Connor being the dick he is, started working with the most horrendous man on the planet. A hunter... he killed my whole pack when I was younger, I was the only survivor. I had no idea he had survived the attack until he kidnapped me...

You heard me right, he kidnapped me, and Connor helped him hold me for weeks.

Despite their efforts to bring me home, Logan and Alexi were too late. I was severely injured and no longer able to heal. Doctors said I was in a coma and would never wake up. However, once again the Goddess was on our side, because despite all odds I awoke.

That's my story, or the short version anyway. So here I am settling into my reading chair at the pack house, my handsome mate fast asleep on the bed in front of me. Everything crazy I have experienced over the past two months has been worth it because I will spend the rest of my life with him.

Until two months ago, all I wanted to do was run away from this pack; now the idea of leaving is horrible. This pack is my home, it is perfect, and I have everything I could ever want.

"Good morning, little one. What are you doing up so early?"

When my eyes found Logan, I couldn't help but stare at him shirtless as he sat there, staring at me with his cheeky grin. I couldn't stop my eyes from drifting downwards, his eight-pack in full view.

When I finally stopped eye fucking my mate, I noticed a smirk playing across his lips, obviously enjoying the attention.

"I couldn't sleep."

A look of concern crossed his face as he crossed the room towards me, wrapping his arms around me. The feeling of being in my mate's arms instantly started calming me.

"What's wrong, Love?"

My stomachache disappeared as he smiled at me. "Nothing, I'm fine. It's been a crazy couple of months. Besides, today I officially become Luna. I don't care for parties or being in the centre of attention."

As he spoke, his expression relaxed: "You don't have to worry, they'll adore you. You were born to lead. Come on, let's get ready and then have breakfast, I asked the omegas to make pancakes."

Goddess I love this man, he truly knows the way to my heart. Smiling from ear to ear as I followed him to the bathroom, to shower with my beast of a mate. Sometimes I really do love my life.

It took an hour for us to finally make it to the dining room, seeing Logan soaped up in all his glory was just plain distracting. It would be impossible to look at Logan Black, six feet of unrelenting muscle, and not be distracted. That man is intoxicating, whenever he is around it's like my brain is clouded in fog.

I was getting used to living in the pack house, even getting into a routine. Alexi and I trained the warriors in the morning, then I spend the afternoon taking care of pack business.

It was a simple routine, but I had grown to love it, however, today is different. This is the first full moon I have seen since I became Logan's mate, that is, the first one during which I have actually been here. Kidnapping and Coma not included. Meaning today is my Luna ceremony, the day I officially become Blue Moon's Luna.

I'm terrified, this pack has avoided me for years, and most of them have pretended like I don't exist since I moved here. Training with the Warriors over the past couple of weeks has been incredible but I'm still nervous. I've been so nervous that my stomach has been aching almost non-stop. I haven't had a lot of time with the rest of the pack, so I'm not sure how they'll react to me. Logan keeps saying they will love me; I just wish I were as confident as he is.

An Omega pulled me from my inner monologue, as she placed a plate of chocolate chip pancakes in front of me. "Morning Luna."

"Morning Megan, these look amazing. Thank you."

She smiled proudly before heading back to the kitchen, I liked Megan. She is very timid and quiet, but rather sweet. Her short hair was cut into a bob that brushed against her bare caramel skin. Her father is one of the warriors I trained, so when he said she wanted a summer job, I offered her a job in the pack house. Despite my repeated attempts to get her to call me Andy, she still calls me Luna.

"Morning guys. Andy, you missed a crazy training session."

As I looked at Alexi, he was sweaty and smelled of death. The house is overrun with boys, I can't wait until Grayson and Alexi find their mates. I'm outnumbered here.

"You stink!"

He rolled his eyes at me but continued his story. "So, Grey goes mad on Damon and destroys him, not that he didn't have it coming, the guy is a tool."

That's an understatement, Damon was Connor's closest friend and just as evil as him. He hated me, well, still hates me. He refuses to even acknowledge that I am there, he is one of the warriors and will not take a single order from me. Alexi wants him punished, but I refuse; if Logan found out, I think he would lock him up with Connor.

"You talking about me behind my back again, Lex?" Grayson jokingly asked as he entered, sporting exactly the same post-exercise look as Alexi. With his stormy grey eyes, black hair that was reminiscent of beautiful silk and his adorable smile, he was one of the most eligible bachelors in the pack. Standing in nothing but grey sweatpants, I could almost hear every woman in the pack house swoon.

As Logan growled beside me, I realised I had been gazing at the gamma for far too long. Alexi laughed at Grayson's discomfort, seeing that Logan looked like he might kill him.

"You have nothing to worry about handsome."

Logan visibly relaxed at my voice, still glaring at

Grayson as he pulled me onto his lap.

Away from my pancakes...

My efforts to move away towards my food only angered my mate, mainly because Grayson had chosen to sit beside me. Goddess why is he so big, I can barely move him!

Alexi was laughing at my struggle, damn traitor. Just sitting there as I starve to death. My glaring only made him laugh harder, and he calls himself my brother.

"You could help me, you know?" I all but sneered at my brother.

"I could." He agreed.

I'm going to wipe that smug smile off of his stupid face as soon as I'm free. I heard Grayson laugh as he realised what was happening, a growl slipped from my lips, instantly silencing the wolf.

"Never get between Andy and food, trust me, dude." Grayson seemed to accept this and went back to his pancakes.

"Handsome, can you please let me go?" Logan gave me a confused look before releasing me from his death grip.

I took one bite of my breakfast before Megan walked in and announced "Luna, it's time to get ready for the ceremony." With one last mournful look at my food, I stood and followed her upstairs.

In addition to planning the whole ceremony, Logan's mother, the former Luna, even picked out my dress, which I have to admit is stunning. A simple red one-shoulder ball gown, it fit me perfectly. My height made it just reach the floor, allowing it to flow behind me as I walked.

Megan had been assigned to do my hair and makeup, after two hours of sitting in the chair with her fussing over me I realised why Luna had picked her. The girl was talented, I can't believe she made me look so elegant. My makeup wasn't over the top, but it was still stunning. The sides of my hair were swirled into a braid, which laid on top of my tamed curls. I don't think I have ever looked so put together before, don't get me wrong I dress up sometimes but nothing like this, nothing so elegant. Smiling from ear to ear I hugged Megan, thanking her.

"You're coming, right? Please say yes, I could use a friend." I begged.

"I do not think I was invited; besides, I do not have anything to wear."

"Don't worry, we can fix that."

Chapter 2

Logan's POV

The past few months have been the best and worst of my life, but when I woke to find Andy curled up reading a book and feeling completely at home it made me feel excited. None of it mattered, it was all worth it, for her.

My mate is perfect, this moment is perfect. The way her eyes light up as she looks at me, the smile that graces her lips as her eyes trail down my body. I will never tire of looking at her, of touching her. I truly will never understand how she thinks herself to be plain, there is nothing remotely ordinary about her.

The feeling of having my mate in my arms is something I could never describe, there are no words good enough. There's nothing that beats that feeling, well maybe one thing... the view of my mate's naked body dripping from the shower above her. No words could describe the vision in front of me, Andy was perfect.

This woman has legs that any woman would kill for and an ass that I can't wait to dig my teeth into. I couldn't help but get distracted; neither a man nor a wolf could resist this woman.

The Beta's Mate

Brushing my fingers across her neck, working my way down until I reached her ass.

I whispered in her ear, "Spread your legs." A smile graced my lips as she did what I asked without an ounce of hesitation.

Leaning down I started kissing her everywhere, starting at her mark I felt her shudder beneath my lips. Growling, I lifted her, holding her ass firmly in place. Andy wrapped her legs around my hips, bringing me closer, her hands finding their way into my hair.

In one swift movement, I turned Andy so that her back was to the wall. My body effectively held her in place, allowing my hands to move freely. Starting at her hips, I was slowly moving my hands towards her core as I roamed her body.

As I pressed two fingers deep into her mouth, pressing in and out slowly, I felt her flex and clench around me. Desiring to hold me in place, her moans only intensified, until I felt her shudder as waves of pleasure overcame her.

As her breathing began to return to normal, her first question reminded me just how perfect my mate is. "You ready for your turn?" she asked.

As she knelt, she smiled and kept her eyes on me while her beautiful mouth descended on my...

"Logan! Get your head out of the clouds and get

back to work!" My mother's voice yelled, calling me out of my flashback, and after realising I was standing in the middle of the ballroom as everyone set up around me, I immediately got to work. Alexi was struggling to keep a straight face; my embarrassment obviously bringing him joy. And I call this man my friend.

"Yes, Logan, get back to work." He whispered to me, giggling to himself.

"Alexi Jackson, stop joking around and try to be useful." Alexi's face paled as he turned to face the angry, she-wolf.

"Sorry Mother."

Chuckling, I picked up a stack of chairs and brought them to the platform, thanking Mrs Jackson silently. I still have no idea how she and my mother had managed to put all of this together so quickly, the whole pack house looked amazing. From the lights strung across the ceiling to the tables piled high with every delicious food imaginable, they were true miracle workers when it came to party planning.

The moment my mother learned Andy woke up in the pack hospital, she immediately began to prepare the ceremony, offering to do everything so Andy could rest. Everything I have learned about my mate makes me think that Andy appreciated that a lot more than she let on. I have watched that girl take down an army single-handed, but I think party planning terrifies her.

After almost two hours, we finally finished, and the room was filled with beautiful music as the guests arrived. Running upstairs to get changed, if I leave Andy to face the crowd alone, I will never hear the end of it.

Where are you? I could almost feel Alexi's fear through the mind link.

Coming now, what's up?

Your mother is screaming at me. I couldn't stop the burst of laughter that came out of me.

I heard that...

By the time I reached Alexi, I had almost stopped laughing, but the fear in his eyes at the thought of my mother had me laughing again.

"Will you stop, it's not funny. She's scary dude." To be fair to him, that is true. My mother is one of the nicest people you will ever meet however I would definitely not advise crossing her.

My mother's annoyed voice instantly stopped our argument.

"Will you boys hurry up!"

Heads bowed low, we walked into the ballroom like disobedient children.

There are only two people in the world my wolf will allow to speak to us that way, we are an alpha after all. His mate and for some unknown reason our mother.

Because she is terrifying...

And you're an alpha wolf...

So is she!

Rolling my eyes at him Andrea's scent washed over me, the past few hours without my mate have felt like an eternity. Not having her by my side was torture. The thought of seeing her again had me practically running towards her scent. The sight that greeted me made me freeze in place. She looked stunning. The red gown hugged her chest perfectly, making her gorgeous curves even more striking. She smiled her perfect smile at me as she walked over. I felt her lips brush my cheek as she leaned in to whisper in my ear.

"Careful, your wolf is showing."

I could hear the satisfaction in her voice, she was enjoying my reaction. The thought only worsened my struggle. It's taking every piece of self-restraint I have to not throw her over my shoulder and show her just what I think about that dress.

Just wait until after the party, little one.

My smile widened as I watched her cheeks redden, this is going to be fun.

"Andrea, you look stunning my dear."

Mrs Jackson's timing was as always impeccable, she took one look at Andy and rolled her eyes at me.

"Leave my poor daughter alone, just for one evening Logan. Tonight, she belongs to the pack, not just to you."

Chapter 3

Alexi's POV

Watching my sister become Luna is one of the proudest moments in my life. I have always known she was going to be more than just another wolf, ever since we kids, she has been extraordinary. She is an extraordinary person. It is no different tonight.

I know she is nervous, but you would never guess that by looking at her. The whole pack is in awe of her, of what she has survived. Once Connor was locked away, the poison he had inflicted on the pack slowly dissipated.

Everyone started looking at Andy, started taking notice of her. For whom she is, not for how Connor described her.

My mother caught me from my thoughts with, "Hey sweetie.".

Her face lit up as I said, "Hey, you did an incredible job. This place looks great!".

"Thank you, I'm just happy that she's doing so well. She deserves all of this." I smiled, keeping my eyes on Andy and Logan. It's evident just how much Andy means to him by the way his eyes light up when she walks into the room. He would kill for her in a heartbeat. And I'm jealous of him, of how connected they are.

As embarrassing as it is to admit, I am lonely, and I can't wait to find my soul mate. To have the kind of bond they have.

My mother whispered to me, "You'll find your mate."

"How did you know?"

"A mother always knows."

There has been no slowing down whatsoever since the party began hours ago. After everything that's happened over the last few months, the pack deserves a good time.

Andy and Logan are still enjoying themselves, dancing with the rest of the pack.

We have a problem. Grayson's voice invaded my thoughts.

What's happening?

A pack has been attacked; they're asking for our aid.

Which pack?

Silvercrest.

I must have heard him wrong; they would never ask for our help. Silvercrest is notorious for its isolation, as no outsider has been allowed on their lands for decades.

Are you sure it's Silvercrest?

There was a slight pause before he replied.

It is definitely Silvercrest.

I'm on my way, I'll meet you in my office.

Both my office and my bedroom are located on the third floor. The Alpha and Luna had the top floor to themselves, while me and Grayson shared the third floor. Leaving the second for the visiting Alpha's and any omegas who lived in the pack house.

As I entered my office, Grayson was sitting in one of the chairs waiting for me.

"Tell me everything."

Once Grayson had finished talking, I sat down at my desk. Lost for words. Silvercrest asking us for help, the idea is insane. I have only heard my dad mention them once. He hated their alpha, he called him an outdated waste of power. Not worthy of his title.

The only reason it stuck with me was because my father never really had a bad word to say about anyone.

"Should we get Logan?"

"No, let them enjoy tonight. I'll tell them in the morning."

Grayson nodded before standing up and re-joining the party.

Silvercrest can wait for a night, the pack needs this.

We all do.

The rest of the night past by without a hitch. The whole pack enjoyed themselves, even Megan started to have fun. Mostly because Andy refused to let her avoid the party. Never get between Andrea and her target. You will not win.

My sister is a machine.

She will always do everything in her power to help those around her.

Chapter 4

Andy's POV

Beep…

Beep…

Moaning I reached over and hit my alarm clock, 7am.

Goddess I hate morning workouts. Logan pulled me towards him, putting his head in my neck.

"I have to go handsome."

"Skip it." He said, his voice ruff and deep from sleeping.

"I can't I already skipped yesterday."

He groaned as I got out of the bed, unhappy with my answer.

By 7:30 I was in the training arena, helping Alexi and Grayson clear the arena for training.

"Good morning, *Luna*." A male voice drew my attention to the opposite side of the room, to an emotionless Damon. His brown eyes narrowed as he walked towards us.

The guy is such a dick, I still have no idea why you won't just punish him.

Alexi's voice rang through my head, I know he's right. I should deal with Damon, but if I do Logan will be pissed. Connors been locked in the cells since he attacked me, if Logan finds out about Damon, he will throw him down there as well. As much as I dislike the guy, I don't want him imprisoned for having a shitty friend.

I tore my gaze back down to the ground, avoiding Damon's glare.

"I'll take them for a run to warm up." Grayson said as he jogged towards the warriors. I could feel Alexi tensing beside me, as he shuffled on his feet.

Weird.

"What's up Lex?"

He palmed the back of his neck, sighing before he spoke.

"A pack has been attacked by rogues; they are asking for our help."

I stared at my brother; I know him well enough to know that wasn't the whole story. There's no way he would be this nervous about a random pack.

Putting my hands on my hips I waited for my brother.

"It's Silvercrest."

Wait what?

That's not possible.

"Seriously? No one's even heard from them in over a decade."

He nodded his head, before continuing.

"Do you know anything about them?"

I thought about it for a second before replying, did I know anything?

"Only a little, my mother told me about them when I was a kid. She said the alpha was an anachronistic idiot, who should have never been an alpha. And that the whole pack secluded themselves from the world when his mate died."

Alexi visibly paled, shaking his head he whispered. "Damn, that's horrible."

"Yeah, after that Silvercrest never reached out to another pack again."

"Until now, maybe it's because they have a new Alpha. I mean his son should have taken over the title by now."

Alexi was right, his son should be in his twenty's now. I don't know much about him; I just hope he's nothing like his father.

"Who are you thinking of sending?"

Alexi thought about it for a second before answering me. "I was thinking maybe us and Logan. Grayson's more than capable of running this place for a few days, if we leave in the morning we can hopefully be back by the weekend."

Before I could respond the doors to the arena opened, pulling our attention as a few dozen warriors flooded the room. I scanned the wolves filling the space, they all looked rough. Apparently, I'm not the only one who drank too much last night. Chuckling I walked over to Grayson who stood at the front of the group, appearing completely unfazed.

Either Grayson can seriously hold were wine or he didn't have nearly enough fun last night.

A slow smile pulled at Alexi's lips.

I think you're right little sister.

"Everyone pair up, we're doing one on one's today."

I was met with a chorus of 'yes Luna's' as they all paired off, myself Lex and Grayson split up. Each of us taking a corner, watching the warriors fight.

A deep growl filled the air, I spun around to see a pissed off Damon standing over a bloodied warrior. The warrior looked half dead; I couldn't quite remember his name. Thomas, I think. Damon growled again, moving closer to Thomas baring his fangs.

"What the hell are you doing Damon?"

Ignoring me, the enraged wolf prowled closer.

Oh, hell no, there is no way I'm allowing him to attack an unconscious man. My anger began to boil over, heat flooded my chest and without looking I knew my arms were engulfed in flames. Damon paused, looking at me. A smirk covered his face. "Can't beat me without your little tricks *Luna*?"

A swirl of anger rippled through my core, extinguishing the flames I stalked closer to him.

"Want to bet?" I taunted.

A smile covered his face as he stalked towards me. The other warriors formed a circle around us, excited for a show.

"Now this little wolf is going to be fun." He sneered before lunging for me.

Blocking him at the last second, I got the satisfaction of watching him stumble before catching his footing. The room filled with the sound of laughter as the wolves all cheered.

I couldn't help but laugh with them, the look of pure unfiltered hatred on Damon's face had my heart racing. I have no idea why he gets to me so much, it's not like I can't take him. I've not had anyone hate me like that since Connor. Noticing my hesitation Damon lunged for me again, this time tackling me to the ground. Regaining myself I hurl him off of me, he landed with a loud thud before growling again.

"What the hell is your problem?"

"You are, everywhere you go death follows you."

Standing there in shock, I couldn't find the right words to say. What did he mean? What does death have to do with me?

Although my only desire has always been to protect those I love, a part of me believes he is right. Maybe I've been doing this wrong all along. Maybe he's right.

"Shut the hell up Damon. You have no idea what you are talking about." Alexi screamed, his anger flowing freely.

Throughout my life, my brother has protected me, even when there was no need for it. The silence in the arena was broken by Damon's growling before he left the arena. The warriors around us went back to training, keeping their eyes away from us.

"Ignore him, little sister, he has no clue what he's talking about."

Alexi tried his best to console me, but it wasn't working. Demon had exploited my greatest insecurities. This idea that I might pose a threat to this pack. The fact that he made it feel real made me realize I wasn't the only one thinking it, that maybe the rest of the pack was as well. I walk through with my head lowered, leaving my brother and Grayson to finish training. There was no way I could face them, no way I could pretend it didn't affect me. If I were a better actor, maybe my life would be a bit different. But as it stands, I just couldn't face it.

If Damon was only angry because he was afraid, are they all afraid of me? I have been trying to avoid using my power because it is so unstable and honestly it terrifies me. If I used it again, what if I burnt another pack to the ground!! I am not strong enough to lose another family.

I missed my mother more than anything else for the first time in years. Before I knew it, I was walking through their house. My ears filled with the sound of my mother singing off key to the radio and my father screaming at the football. As soon as I saw my mother, I immediately calmed, a sense of home overtook me. She smiled when she saw me for the first time. Her smile disappeared, covering her face with worry.

"Are you okay sweetie?"

Without saying a word, I wrapped my arms around

her, the smell of flowers filling my nose. She hugged me to her, kissing the top of my head as she held me there. A few seconds later another pair of arms wrapped around us, and I knew my father had come in. Not caring about missing his game.

"What happened sweetie?" my mum asked releasing her hold on me. I looked up at my parents, taking a deep breath I told them everything that happened in the arena.

When I was done my dad just sighed as he wrapped an arm around me.

"He shouldn't be blaming you for what happened, I'm sorry sweetie."

I just stared at my father, his expression was painful to watch. He was always so calm and happy around us, but he looked defeated.

"Blaming me for what?"

He took a deep breath before answering me.

"For his father."

When I stayed quiet, he continued.

"He was our best warrior, he came with us to Crescent Moon. Whilst we were searching the pack he was jumped by a hunter. By the time we reached him it was too late."

My fathers gaze stayed glued to the floor, obviously not willing to look at us. He had lost one of his men that day and I could tell he blamed himself.

I pulled him in for a hug, wrapping my arms around his neck.

"You didn't do anything wrong, it's not your fault."

He smiled down at me, kissing my forehead he whispered.

"Its not yours either kiddo. I'm sorry he's blaming you."

"Its okay." I said.

And I actually meant it, if hating me helps him feel better about his father I can live with that.

"Who's hungry?" my mother asked, not liking the sadness in her kitchen.

My dad laughed, shaking his head at his mate.

"Have you ever met our daughter? When is she NOT hungry?" mum laughed as I moaned. Dad looked at me, eyebrow raised. "Does that mean you don't want any food?"

I shook my head quickly.

"I could eat."

They both laughed as my mother started cooking. Giving me and dad orders as she prepared the food.

By the time we were eating I had forgotten all about Damon, and just enjoyed spending some time with my parents. I hadn't been able to see a lot of them since I had woken up in the hospital and I didn't realise just how much I missed this feeling of home.

Chapter 5

Connor's POV

Pacing.

All I do is pace this cell, for over a month they have kept me down here. In this dark and putrid place.

My pathetic excuse for a brother, has the nerve to make her his Luna.

How dare he take what's mine.

Rejection or not.

"Hey baby." Tyler's shrill voice pulled me from my thoughts.

Goddess her voice annoys me.

"How you been baby?"

Seriously?

"I'm locked in a cell; how do you think I've been?"

She pouted, what I assume was supposed to be sexy but just came across as childish.

"Don't be mean, I did exactly what you asked Connie."

Ignoring the infuriating nickname, I kept myself and my voice calm.

"Good girl, it won't take them long to act."

Tyler paused for a moment, nervously playing with her hair.

"What is it?"

"Well, I was just wondering why?"

"Why, what?"

"Why you hate her so much." She whispered, staring down at her feet.

Now that is a long story.

10 years ago...

I watched as my brother trained with my father. Same time everyday they would go down to the beach and train, leaving me alone. He always paid more attention to Logan. To the future alpha.

My father had missed the last training, off on some business trip. But he seemed different today, he wasn't himself.

Logan however didn't seem to notice our father's off mood. Sometimes I envied my brother. He knew who he was supposed to be, no worries. He had everything.

The sound of crying pulled my attention. Sitting by the cliff, is a girl, her head in her hands as she sobs. Her golden hair was braided down her back, and her clothes looked oversized and strange on her.

Slowly I made my way towards her, she flinched away as I sat beside her.

"I'm sorry, I didn't mean to scare you."

She raised her face to mine, tears streaked down her face as her eyes met mine.

Her eyes.

They were amazing, blue flames flicked making her already bright eyes look brighter.

"I'm Connor."

She smiled slightly, not reaching her eyes.

"Rea."

We spent the rest of the day playing on the beach, her smile stayed small but for me it was one of the best days of my life.

To my joy, Rea agreed to meet me the next day.

For days we met on the cliffs, spending the day playing in the sand.

One day I got back to the packhouse to find my mother cooking dinner, she smiled down at me as I walked in the kitchen.

"What's got you looking so happy mister?"

"I think I met my mate, and she's perfect."

My mother stops and looks at me, her face breaking into a brilliant smile.

"That's amazing news, what's her name?"

"Rea Hale."

My mothers face fell as I spoke.

"I'm sorry sweetie, but she's not your mate."

A strange feeling overwhelmed me, pain. Like everything hurt at the same time.

"Why?"

She looked like she was deciding what to say carefully.

"She's Logan's mate sweetie, I'm sorry."

Logan!

How can he have her as well!

He can't have her, she's mine.

How can he have her?

It's not fair, he's just an idiot with a sword.

She likes me, I know it.

The next morning, I ran to the beach eager to see Rea again.

The cliff was empty, where is she?

Did she decide not to come?

The sound of giggling catches my attention and I turn to see Logan holding a sword, pretending to dual Rea as she giggles hysterically.

Laughing.

She's laughing with him. The entire time we had spent together she had barely smiled, but a few minutes with him and she's hysterical.

She seemed so happy with him, all nervousness and fear had disappeared.

Why is she so relaxed with him?

She's mine, he can't have her.

"Logan, father wants you." I yelled.

Logan immediately turned and heading to the packhouse, waving a goodbye to Rea.

Rea walked over to me, a smile still covering her face.

"Hi."

I nodded to her and headed for our cliff. We had spent everyday here under the massive oak tree.

"Did I do something wrong?"

Rea whispered, her fear showing through again. Why is she afraid with me but not him?

"Why him?" my voice came out angrier than I had intended, causing her to shrink away.

"I don't understand, he seemed nice." She whimpered.

"Not him, you can't talk to him again."

"Why? He's, my friend."

"I said NO."

Rea huffed, turned and started walking away from me.

"Where are you going?"

"Home."

"Why?"

"Because I don't want to hang out with you anymore."

Her eyes glowed, as the flames flickered again.

"Why not?"

"Because you're mean!" she yelled.

"I am not mean, stop being stupid."

"I am not stupid, and you are mean, telling me who to talk to is mean, yelling at me is mean, calling me stupid is mean."

She goes to walk away again but I follow her until she stops.

"I don't want to be your friend anymore Connor."

"Who are you going to be friends with then? Because no one else will want a rogue as a friend."

I could see the hurt in her eyes, but I ignored it.

This was her fault.

She yelled before walking away, not even bothering to look back.

"Don't ever talk to me again."

She chose him.

Why would she choose him?

"Connor?" Tyler's voice sounded worried as she waved her hand in front of my face.

When she sighed and left, I went back to pacing, thoughts of my mate filling my head.

When the pack started treating her badly, I didn't stop them, I coached them on. And when my friends started hitting her, I never helped her. Once my wolf showed my anger only intensified, he hated her. He hated her for rejecting us before ever meeting him.

Chapter 6

Alexi's POV

It was a long drive to Silvercrest, by the time we arrived Andy was asleep on Logan's shoulder. I couldn't help but envy my sister, she had found her mate. Jealousy is something that I hate, especially at Andy. I know she senses something is wrong, and I know that it hurts her. My sister, as amazing as she is, keeps it to herself. I hate this, because we talk about everything, but I don't want to burden her with this. She is finally happy, I'm being ridiculous. Moping around because I haven't found my mate, I know she's out there somewhere. I just wish I could finally meet her, seeing how happy Logan and Andy are, is only making the emptiness I feel worse.

I've never been to Silvercrest, though I have heard the rumours. I don't think there's a wolf who hasn't. The pack's famous for being arrogant and old fashioned, most wolves have learned to adapt to the modern world and all its views.

It's rare for Silvercrest to acknowledge other packs, asking for help was unheard of. I know Logan's just as curious as me to see inside their pack, to actually meet their new alpha.

When the car pulled up to the packhouse everything was silent, there were no sounds of nature or children playing. It felt wrong, a pack is normally filled with life. Back home you can always hear the seagulls flying above and the children laughing.

This was the opposite, complete silence.

You can feel that right?

I nodded to Logan as we walked towards the Alpha, he seemed impatient. His foot silently tapping the ground as we approached.

He looked in his late forties, with grey taking over his dark hair and making the wrinkles on his face appear more prominent. Everything about him screamed alpha, from his posture to the power emanating from him.

"Good afternoon, we are from Blue moon. I'm Andy, this is my mate Logan and our beta Alexi." Andy was her usual smiling self, unbothered by the alpha being one herself. Most alpha's, Andy and Logan included rain in their power, to avoid those around them feeling threatened. Making the alpha here even stranger, it was like he wanted to point out his power to us.

The alpha looked towards Logan, ignoring Andy as he spoke. "Michael Novak, my son Erik is the current alpha. He is on patrol, I offered to show you to your rooms. Follow me."

We had to hurry to keep up with his pace as he hurried up two sets of spiral staircases, the inside of the pack house resembling a castle. From the out-dated wallpaper to the expensive handcrafted furniture, whoever lives in this house cares an awful lot about appearances. Nothing is out of place; nothing feels lived in. The whole place looks untouchable, and uncomfortable.

"The first door is the Alpha's suite and the second is the Beta's, if you need anything during your stay just ask the omega's downstairs. Now if you'll excuse me, I have things to attend to."

We all watched him leave, the second he was far enough away Andy broke the silence. "I don't like him; he seems like a dick."

My sister has never been one to hold back, to be honest I completely agree. If that's the alpha's father, what's the alpha like.

"I think you're right; we will have to see what his son is like."

Two hours later, Logan and Andy are in their room and all my things are unpacked. I really need some single friends, I know this isn't a social visit. We are working, but I honestly have nothing to do, sighing I walked out of my empty room.

I love Logan, but I miss my sister. I know she's happy and they're enjoying their time together. I just wish that didn't mean I have to be a third wheel all of the time. Every friend I have has met their mate, Grayson's the only one left who hasn't met his mate, but I barely know him.

I know I have to be patient; fate will eventually bring us together. I just wish fate would hurry up.

Everything in this pack feels weird, everyone I walk past avoids eye contact with me. No one has spoken a single word to me.

If it weren't for the eerie silence and the strange behaviour of the pack members, I would almost think it was beautiful here. The pack was located in the middle of a forest, every direction was lined with trees. There's something comforting about it, like you're in your own world. Completely cut off from everything and everyone, though now I think about it maybe that's not the best thing.

The sound of someone screaming pulled me from my inner monologue. By the time I reached her she was already pulling herself off of the ground, quietly muttering to herself. Paper scattered all around her, covered in mud.

"Are you okay?" my voice came out weaker than I had expected, confusing me.

She jumped, before turning around to face me.

She was beautiful, copper hair cascading across her shoulders, still messy from falling. She was small, compared to me at least, but her green eyes widened, and I froze. Everything about her was perfect, she was everything I never knew I wanted. My wolf howled in my head saying the one word that I had longed to hear.

Mate!

Chapter 7

Verity's POV

"Get up, Verity; breakfast won't make itself." A man shouted while banging on my door.

Rolling over I read my clock, 9am.

Crap!

I overslept; he's going to kill me. Grabbing jeans and a t-shirt, I made my way downstairs, avoiding running into anyone. How could I be so stupid? I forgot to set my alarm. In a flash I fried some eggs and bacon and put the last plate of breakfast in the dining room just as the pack members started pouring in.

Sighing, I started cleaning the kitchen, but before I could finish the sound of growling stopped me in my tracks, the sound always sent shivers down my spine. Turning I saw Erick standing in the doorway, his eyes a deadly shade of black.

"I... I'm almost finished." My voice came out barely above a whisper. He took a step towards me, a smile covering his lips when I shifted away from him. The counter pressed up against my back as he continued to edge closer to me, enjoying my fear.

I have never understood why he hates me so much; he takes so much pleasure from my pain, it terrifies me. Everyone else showed some guilt. Never him. He always punishes me. He has never shown any mercy to me. There's nothing I can do though, I'm stuck here. in my own personal hell, surrounded by people who hate me for being born. All anyone here does is remind me that I should never have existed in the first place.

Putting an arm on either side of me, he trapped me against the counter. I watched as he grabbed the plate of food, I had left behind me, for myself to eat. A smirk covered his lips as he threw the plate across the room, the sound of it crashing against the wall making me flinch.

"Why did you make me do that? You know the rules, you feed us, not yourself."

Not trusting my voice, I simply nodded.

"You know that I have to punish you now, we can't have anyone thinking I am taking it easy on you." With that he grabbed me by my arm and threw me, as easily as he had thrown the food. My side hit the wall with a deafening crack, and I knew I broke a rib. Pain shot through me as he lifted me up, I took a deep breath as I brought my eyes up to meet his. But instead, I was met with his fist. Why is this my life?

What did I do to deserve this?

A whimper escaped my lips as my world went black.

Pain.

Why am I in pain?

Right, Erick. Moaning I sat up, I'm back in my room. At least he didn't just leave me there this time, I guess having your omega bleeding on the floor wouldn't look good, especially to the Alpha visiting today.

I caught a glimpse of myself in the mirror, God I look awful. Sighing I made my way to the shower, glaring at the running water. Might as well get it over with, a whimper left my lips as the hot water cascaded over my wounds. I was weak, I have always been weak. My body takes longer to heal than normal wolves, most would have started to heal already. But not me, I'm one of the lucky ones. I suppose I should be grateful that I still heal, even if it is slower than normal. Otherwise, my entire body would be covered in scars.

Thanking the goddess that my face wasn't swollen, I applied the lightest amount of makeup, just enough to cover the bruises. Taking a look at my alarm clock, I realized I had slept through the whole day. At least I don't have to cook dinner.

Putting on some jeans and a hoodie, not bothering

to dry my hair. Grabbing my sketchpad, I left my little bedroom and made my way out of the house. That however is where my luck ended, Sam was standing in the middle of the kitchen, blocking my exit.

"So nice of you to join us Vivi, just where do you think you are going?"

Sam is another of my main tormentors, being Erick's beta, he has always followed his lead.

"For a walk." I tried to push around him, but he didn't budge.

"Sam, just leave her alone." I turned to see a terrified Molly, her hand over her mouth. She looked in shock, to be honest so was I. No one has ever stood up for me before. What was even more shocking is that she's Sam's mate, I still have no idea how someone so sweet got mated to this monster.

"What did you just say to me?" Sam's voice came out as a growl, making Molly flinch away.

"I... I'm sorry, I didn't mean to. Please, I'm sorry."

I watched frozen in place as Sam gripped his helpless mate by the throat, his eyes shifting to black as he lifted her above the ground.

"I... didn't m...mean." Molly's cries were barely audible.

I can't watch this, but my whole body is frozen. I can't look away, why can't I look away.

A growl I didn't recognise pulled my attention; it was a she wolf. Her blue eyes almost appeared to glow in the dimly lit room as she made her way over to the fighting couple. I watched stunned as she lifted Sam as if he weighed nothing. Her anger came off of her in waves as she approached him, grabbing his neck, and copying his actions.

"You stupid bitch, who do you think you are." He managed to choke out between breaths. His words only made her smile, I couldn't find any fear in her eyes. How is she doing that, how is she standing up to a beta like that. An omega shouldn't be able to beat a beta in a fight, it's not possible.

"Who do you think you are?" she growled, tightening her hand around his neck. "Who gave you the right to beat someone smaller than you? Does it make you feel like a man?" Sam's eyes widened in shock at her words, as he tried to get free from her grip.

"You are a pathetic excuse for a wolf, touch her again and I will kill you." Tossing him to the floor, she scowled down at him. Molly whimpering caught her attention, making her rush to the wounded girl crumpled up on the floor.

"What the hell is going on here?" Not him, the anger in his voice had my skin crawling, and I ran.

I'm not proud of it, but what can I do? I couldn't stay there and watch her get punished, it's not like I could stand up to him. He's an alpha and I'm nothing.

Once I reached the lake I could barely breathe, it had been years since I ran so fast. I tried to relax, to focus on my sketch, but nothing worked. I couldn't shut my thoughts off.

Why did she do it? Why would she do something so stupid? How did she beat him, he's a beta?

We are not built to fight, and it's the first thing they teach us. I must be crazy; no female could face a male wolf.

My father told me the story of my birth when I was a pup, my mother had a difficult pregnancy and one night she started to go into labour. Only it was too early, I was too early. My mother died giving birth to me, I never got the chance to meet her. My father blamed me; correction blames me. If it weren't for me his mate would still be alive, he would be happy. From what I have heard, the death of a mate is the worst pain imaginable. Most wolves don't survive it.

The doctors thought I wouldn't survive the night, but against all odds here I am. Lucky me. The fact that I was born a runt, don't have a wolf, and can't shift made it impossible for me to have a mate. I'm weaker because of it; I've always been weak. Mates should be two wolves finding each other, but since I have no wolf, I'm likely to have no mate.

After losing interest in sketching, I made my way back to the pack house. So much for relaxing and taking my mind off of everything. I swear, I have no luck in life. My guardian angel is on vacation. Like the universe is trying to prove me right, I trip over my own feet. Screaming in the girliest voice of my life. Seriously? Why the hell does this crap happen to me?

"God damn it, why me?" I mutter as I brush the mud from my jeans. My pleas to the universe unsurprisingly did not receive any response. I really need to leave this place, maybe by getting out I will be able to hide among humans. Since after all, I am mostly human. Although I do not think my father will ever allow me to leave.

"Are you okay?"

I couldn't help the yelp that left me, dear god what is wrong with me? Turning around, my eyes fell on the most gorgeous man I have ever met. Six feet of muscle with bright blue eyes and messy brown hair, my heart started to beat faster. The second our eyes met one word came to my mind, the one word I thought was impossible all these years.

Mate.

Chapter 8

Andy's POV

Silvercrest was not what I expected, everything here felt stuck. Everything in the room looked as though it was from decades ago, as if someone had no desire to move on. Nothing here actually resembles a home, honestly it was unsettling. Even the room we had been given felt wrong, almost as if it should be covered in dust in some abandoned building. What happened to make a pack act so weird, what happened to take the life out of this pack.

"You okay there little one?" Logan's worry was only too apparent in his voice, making my face brighten. how did I get so lucky to find someone so concerned about me?

"I'm fine, this place just feels weird. Can you feel it?" As I put my arms around his shoulders, Logan pulled me onto his lap before responding. "Lifeless? The whole place feels lifeless."

"Yes, it makes me feel uncomfortable. Especially that Alpha, he refused to acknowledge me at all."

"My wolf didn't like it. I had to keep him in check so he wouldn't attack the guy."

Smiling, I leant down and kissed him. "Thank you, handsome."

"Anytime, baby." He whispered, pulling me closer.

As I ran my hands underneath his shirt, I felt him growl in my mouth as I repositioned myself with a leg on either side of him.

After two extremely satisfying hours, I'm curled up in bed with my naked mate next to me. Why can't I sleep when everything is amazing? I cannot shake the feeling that something is wrong about this place. With a sigh, I gave up. While I untangled myself from Logan, I decided to take a walk, hoping that would help me to sleep.

Even though it was only eight pm, the house was still eerily quiet as I made my way downstairs. A loud yelling stopped me in my tracks as I approached the front door. The noise piqued my curiosity and I walked toward it. My blood was boiling when I saw what was in front of me, and a growl escaped my lips before I could control it.

A man stood, his hand wrapped around the throat of a woman, lifting her in the air as she struggled.

She was pleading with him. "I... didn't mean." She looked terrified, and my heart broke when I saw the look in her eyes. She looked hopeless, as though she had given up long ago.

I saw another girl with the same terrified expression from the corner of my eye. The woman's back was pressing against the wall as if she were frozen in place.

I've had enough, I'm going to break his neck. While he looked shocked when I lifted him off of her, the surprise was soon replaced by anger. Then I mimicked his actions by grasping his neck and holding him off the floor as he struggled to free himself.

"You stupid bitch, who do you think you are." He managed to choke out between breaths. As I smiled, I could feel my wolf trying to get out, begging me to end it. To show this pathetic little man who we are, but I resisted. We don't need a war between our packs.

"Who do you think you are?" I growled at him, tightening my hand around his neck. "Who gave you the right to beat someone smaller than you? Does it make you feel like a man?" His eyes widened in shock at my words, and I could tell my eyes had changed. Instantly he started to freak out, trying to get away from me.

"You're a pathetic excuse for a wolf, touch her again and I'll kill you." Throwing him to the ground, the girl's sobs caught my attention, and I rushed to her as she lay crumpled on the floor.

"What the hell is going on here?"

Turning I was met with the Alpha's angry eyes, well the former Alpha. He growled at me as he stood in the doorway, his eyes pitch black. The sound reverberated through the building, making the girl next to me whimper in terror.

"I asked a question, Sam!" he growled out.

Sam turned and bowed his head in submission, "She came out of nowhere Alpha, she's crazy."

It took me a moment to realise that he meant me, that son of a bitch. How can he possibly think he will get away with that, he must be an idiot? Before looking down at the whimpering girl, the Alpha turned his gaze back on me.

The girl looked up at him, tears falling from her eyes. "Apologise Molly and I will let you leave." he said. After walking over to Sam, she stood looking at him bowing her head and in a whispered sob said. "I'm sorry, I shouldn't have said that."

Why would she do that? I couldn't believe it. "He's a dick. Don't apologise to him." He deserves everything he got.

Michael spoke up before Sam could defend himself. "He's, her mate; he may do as he pleases".

My anger was building up again. Did he just say mate? The scumbag is not going to get away with strangling his mate. After charging at him, I felt myself get jerked back with such force that my back hit a counter with a deafening crack.

Michael glared at me, "You need to learn your place. You're attacking my Beta." He started to storm towards me, his eyes turning black as he started to shift. I began to shift as well before a growl brought me back to my senses and I met Logan's eyes.

It was clear that he was pissed, and his wolf was struggling to emerge as he ran towards the attacking Alpha, positioning himself between us.

Logan growled loudly, using every ounce of his alpha tone. "You touch her again, and I'll kill you." The couple in the corner flinched and turned away from the enraged Alpha.

After calming his wolf, Michael turned to Logan. "You need to keep your bitch under control, I will not allow anyone to disrespect my pack. She must learn her place."

Logan's growl echoed throughout the house, "You need to watch your mouth, and so do your pack. Andrea is an Alpha, and you will treat her as one." I instinctively reached for my mate, feeling him calm a little under my touch.

My own anger subsided as I looked at my mate. As he listened to his words, Michael tensed. What's wrong with this guy?

"I will not allow her to attack my pack members."

he spat.

While I tried to ignore it, it was obvious that he was barely looking at me. He only acknowledged me when he glared at me. Despite Logan's tensing, I knew he wouldn't be able to hold back his wolf for long. No matter how much I would like to see this Alpha put in his place, we are not here to fight them. It's important to at least try to avoid a war with them, I really hate this Luna stuff sometimes. If it were a year ago, he would be unconscious already.

It's okay Logan, just let it go. I mind linked him before he was able to attack. It was clear that Michael knew we were talking as he stared at us with a patient expression.

He disrespected you, and you want me to just let it go? I could hear the anger in his voice. Although I didn't want to hurt my mate, how could I put my pack at risk because he hurt my feelings...

Logan, please. I pleaded.

I felt Logan relax before he murmured, "If you talk to my mate like that again, I will kill you, but she will not attack anyone else." Logan walked out of the room, not even sparing a glance at me.

He will understand. My wolf spoke up, but I could feel her pain as well. Our mate was pissed at us.

Michael threw a smirk over his face, as if he had somehow won the argument. We had overlooked the couple's exit from the room, but they had left without even looking back. Leaving the room, I started making my way back to ours; I couldn't be in the same room as that arsehole and not make a bad decision.

I felt worse when I found the room empty. Where is he?

Chapter 9

Alexi's POV

I've finally found her, I cannot believe it; I have finally found my soulmate. Her beauty is unparalleled, and she is without a doubt the most stunning woman I have ever seen in my life. I had to stop myself from joining in as my wolf howled with joy. When I reached out to touch her cheek, I felt my heart break when she flinched away.

Whimpering echoed through my mind, as my wolf contemplated the simple gesture.

In an instant, her eyes clouded over as she stepped back, her face etched with fear.

My mate was terrified.

The sight of it caused me to growl. She took another step back, gasping.

Damnit, I'm already failing at this.

"I'm sorry, are you okay?"

Her eyes filled with questions as she looked up at me before she whispered.

"I have to go."

As soon as I was about to protest, she turned and ran toward the house.

What just happened?

What are you doing! My wolf howled.

What?

Mate is scared, and you're letting her leave you idiot.

It's so damn annoying when he's right. As I chased after her, he huffed at me. When I reached the pack house, there was no sign of her. Where is she? I've already lost her... How did that happen...

"Hey Lex, where have you been?"

Andy's voice brought me back to reality and as I stood there staring at her, I had no idea how to respond. She looked at me with worry etched on her features as she sensed my panic.

"What is it? What happened?"

When I took a deep breath, I explained everything that had happened, including finding my mate and seeing her runaway scared. Andy sat quietly by my side, listening intently. Her face lit up with a smile as she took in everything she had just heard. As she pulled me close, she whispered. "Lex, you found her! That's amazing."

My eyes were wide open as I stared at her, confused.

"I'm not saying that it couldn't have gone better, but you've found her."

She's right, she's always right.

All these years she was here, so close to me all this time. I waited for her for so long, and damn was she worth it.

"There is just one question I have for you." Andy said.

She looked up at me with her eyebrows raised and her head shaking.

"Why in the goddamn hell are you talking to me when your mate is here and scared? Find her, you idiot."

Told you...

Hugging her I ran out of the room, to my mate.

Two hours, that is how long I've been searching for her. I don't understand how she could just disappear. Why didn't I stop her from leaving?

Because you are a moron. My wolf howled at me, for the tenth time. I can't say I blame him; I did lose our mate within minutes of meeting her.

The smell of cookie dough stopped me in my tracks, she's here. Searching through the dimly lit garden my eyes finally landed on a mess of bright Cooper curls. She was sitting on the bench furthest from the house, her head hung low in her hands. Her quiet sobs echoed in the small garden; with every cry I felt my heart breaking even more.

Slowly I walked towards her, keeping my footsteps as light as I could. Watching her closely I sat beside her, she jumped as I sat. Only now noticing I was here, strange.

"Are you okay?"

Without looking at me she replied, her voice so quiet I almost didn't understand her.

"I'm fine, you don't have to check up on me."

Resisting the urge to wrap her in my arms and protect her from the world, I decided to just speak the truth.

"It's my job to check up on you, to be honest I've been searching for you for years. There's no way I'm giving up when I've finally found you."

Turning to me, my eyes met hers. And for the second time in my life, the world around me disappeared. Nothing else mattered, just her.

The slightest smile spread across her face as she looked at me, making my heartbeat rapidly.

Her voice whispered out, echoing through my mind as I memorised the sound.

"I don't even know your name."

"Alexi."

"Alexi." She repeated, as if testing it on her tongue.

My name sounded amazing coming from her, I wanted to hear her say it again.

"Mine is Verity."

"Verity." I repeated, copying her. Her cheeks reddened as I spoke, even her name is beautiful.

"Do you live in the packhouse?"

She stayed silent for a minute before nodding, her eyes never looking up from the floor.

"You're from the visiting pack?"

"Yeah, Blue Moon. I'm the beta."

She straightened up, her face going emotionless, before standing. Copying her I stood up, waiting to find out what was going on.

Her eyes locked on mine again, they widened as if she only just realised, I had followed her.

"I'm sorry, it's getting late, I should get back."

I didn't want her to leave but I know I can't just

make her stay with me, nor do I want to order her about. She is my mate, my equal.

"Okay but meet me here tomorrow. At sunset."

Pausing for a moment, she seemed to think it through before whispering. "Okay." And running back to the house.

Chapter 10

Andy's POV

After Lexi left, I was left alone with my thoughts. So much had happened in just a couple of days, and now was a perfect time to sort out my feelings. I knew at any moment Logan could be coming back and I have no idea what I'm going to say.

I hate that Logan is mad at me, but what else could I have done. Our pack comes first, no matter what. I had promised to protect them, to help lead them. How could my first act as Luna be to start a pointless war. My stomach turned once again, and for the second time in two days I had to go to the bathroom. Only just making it to the toilet before throwing up, just missing the tiled floor.

Pulling myself off the floor I showered, washing the events of the day off my skin. The warm water soothed my sore muscles, allowing my mind to drift again.

I still cannot believe Alexi has found his mate; I know the past few weeks have been hard on him. I have spent so much time with Logan, I should have done a better job at being a sister.

By the time I had dried off and changed I only felt

more worried, Logan had not come back yet.

Where is he?

I don't know Doll. I could hear the worry in my wolf's voice as she responded.

Where is our mate?

I fell asleep alone for the first time since I found Logan.

After gently waking, I felt soft rays of sunlight touch my face. I slowly opened my eyes to find Logan's emerald eyes staring back at me.

Goddess, he is gorgeous. It still does not seem possible that he's mine.

"Good morning, little one." He said with a husky voice. There was a hint of sadness in his eyes.

Snuggling into him, I replied, "Good morning."

The beautiful smile that spread across his face made my heart swell. My gaze followed his lips down to his bare chest as I was mesmerised by him.

The low growl from deep within Logan's chest caught my attention, and I turned back to him.

Then he smirked, "I can smell you, little one.

What's going on in that dirty mind of yours?"

No matter how many times we have played this game, my cheeks warmed under his gaze. He still makes me blush whenever he stares at me like that. Like he is a starving man, and I am his last meal.

I whispered, "I'm thinking about you, your hands, roaming every inch of me.".

Within seconds Logan's eyes flashed black before he captured my lips in a blazing kiss.

With one arm wrapped around my waist Logan brought the other up to cup the back of my head. Pulling me impossibly closer he bit down on my lip, causing me to gasp.

Before I knew it, his tongue had found its way into my mouth. He tasted like the sweetest caramel, instantly I became addicted.

He was the first to break the kiss, causing me to let out a whimper. I needed him, wanted him. Leaning up on his elbows, hovering above me he gave me the sexiest smirk before his face went more serious.

"I'm sorry, Little One, I shouldn't have been so mad at you."

Using my index finger, I traced the side of his cheek, trying to memorise every inch of him. As he leaned into my touch, he let out a sigh of relief, letting go of all the weight he had been carrying.

"It's okay, I hated doing it. I wanted to hurt him so bad, but I could not. We can't."

I was interrupted by Logan before I could finish. "I know, I understand. It was a lot harder than I thought it would be, for the first time in my life being Alpha is not my first thought. You are and watching him throw you across the room made me snap."

Pulling him towards me I brought his lips to mine, pouring everything I have into the kiss. Showing him just how much I love him; just how much I need him.

Leaning into my kiss we forgot about everything around us, the whole world drifted away as we got lost in each other.

My entire body needed him, all I wanted in that moment was him. Nothing else mattered to me, not now, not ever. He is my entire world; I could not survive without him.

Logan's hands roamed my body finding their way to my core with ease. A moan escaped my lips as Logan's fingers entered me, slowly. Almost teasing me with their movements. My nails dug into Logan's back causing a growl to erupt from his chest.

His fingers increased in speed making a moan slip from my lips. Within minutes the room filled with the sounds of moaning as an orgasm hit me with the force of an atomic bomb.

As I began to come down from my glorious high, Logan ran his tongue over my mark. Sending sparks all over my body, prolonging my ecstasy.

My body went completely limp.

"How are you feeling, baby?"

"Amazing, nothing could make this moment better." I replied, as my eyes began to drift closed.

I felt him shift and move off the bed, opening my eyes I watched as he started to get dressed. Raising my eyebrow at him, he smirked at me.

"And where do you think you're going handsome?"

"To get my baby pancakes."

Goddess I love this man.

Jumping of the bed I got dressed in a flash as my mate chuckled at me. "I don't think I've ever seen you move so fast little one."

"I'd do anything for pancakes." I replied, walking out of the door.

I only made it a couple of steps before Logan grabbed me, flinging me over his shoulder. From my upside-down vantage point, I could see that he was heading for the kitchen.

"I can walk you know!"

I felt a sharp slap on my ass, which made me moan out loud. Two omegas looked at me, confusion covering their features. My cheeks reddened from embarrassment as Logan chuckled beneath me.

Goddesses kill me.

"If you keep wiggling that delicious ass in my face, I'll do a lot more than just make you moan, little one."

This man is going to be the death of me.

Logan was still chuckling at my embarrassment when we got to the dining hall, he is going to pay for that one later.

As we sat at an empty table, an omega brought us our breakfast. I have no idea who the cook is here, but it smells amazing, I could not resist licking my lips before attacking the massive plate of food.

"You done, little one?"

Nodding, I stood up with Logan and followed him outside. The house seemed slightly more alive than yesterday, though only slightly.

"Where are we going?"

Logan gripped my hand in his and slowed his pace, allowing me to catch up to him.

"I thought we could explore a bit, before the meeting."

Pulling him down for a kiss, I agreed, and we left. The pack lands are beautiful, surrounded by endless forests. It was not long before we found a pond hidden away in the trees.

"It's crazy to think this place can be so beautiful." I whispered.

Logan nodded his agreement as he sat beside the water.

Before I could reach him, a loud splash drew my attention to the water before half the pond splashed onto Logan.

"Tom, stop that this instant." A woman yelled from behind us. She stopped as she took in Logan's-soaked form in front of her.

Stuttering she tried to apologise. "I... I am so sorry. Please, my son is only a boy."

As if being summoned Tom walked out of the water, looking at the ground in shame.

I could not help myself, I burst with laughter. Logan's expression changed as he joined me laughing at himself.

The boy looked at us confused, his chubby cheeks shining red with embarrassment. Resting my hand on his shoulder, I tried my best to reassure him.

"It's okay, we're not mad. Honestly, he needed a shower." Logan grunted at my words.

Logan made a show of shaking his entire body dry, drenching the two of us in the process. As the boy tried his hardest to hold back a giggle, his face instantly lit up. Finally, the boy burst into the cutest giggle I had ever heard, making me laugh again and making me fall in love with him. His big eyes, curly black hair, and chubby cheeks made him one of the cutest kids I've ever seen.

"Tom, we have to get back." The woman spoke, I had completely forgotten she was here. Tom's face fell slightly as he nodded and walked towards her.

Before they left the woman turned to Logan, "Thank you, Alpha. I sincerely apologise for Tom's behaviour; I will make sure this never happens again."

I watched the two of them walk away before I felt a pair of strong arms wrap around me.

"You were amazing with him." I said to Logan.

"I've always loved kids; I've always wanted to be a dad."

I looked at Logan in shock, his eyes went big, and

he tried to back track. "I, I mean someday. It doesn't have to be now, if you want to wait that's fine, I swear."

It was adorable watching him struggle.

"Kids sound good to me."

Logan's smile warmed my heart, he truly is my perfect man. Wrapping me in his arms he flung me over his shoulder again.

"I really can walk you know?"

Ignoring my protests Logan began walking towards the pack house.

"Let's get back we have pups to make."

Chapter 11

Alexi's POV

What made me tell her to meet me at sunset?

It's only noon and I'm already going crazy; all I want to do is see her. Without her, I feel empty, like a piece of me was missing. The entire morning has been spent pacing my suite, trying to convince my wolf not to go find her.

She's our mate, we should be with her.

We will be, I don't want to scare her by stalking her. It was almost impossible to hear the knocking at the door over the growling in my head.

"Lex, you in there?" Andy called through the door.

As I opened the door, she scanned the room, disappointment evident on her face as she asked. "Where is she? I thought she'd be here, I wanted to meet her."

It took me a second to figure out who the 'her' was, sighing as I sat on my bed before answering her question.

"No idea, I managed to find her yesterday, but she ran off again. She agreed to meet me tonight though, but waiting is killing me."

Andy sat beside me, wrapping an arm around my shoulders, instantly calming me down.

"I know it sucks, but it's only a few more hours."

Though I know she's right, I can't help but feel this way. Something feels wrong, something isn't right.

Without realising it, I voiced my greatest fear.

"What if she doesn't show up?""

An expression of sadness crossed her face before she spoke.

"Don't think like that Lex, any girl would be lucky to have you."

Andy grabs my face in her hands when I do not respond, forcing me to look at her.

"Alexi Jackson, listen to me. You are a good man, and she will love you."

There was so much determination in her eyes, I couldn't help but believe her.

"Okay, I believe you."

"Good, now get dressed. We have a meeting to get to." Andy said as she pushed me off the bed.

Smiling I changed into something more meeting worthy than sweatpants and a t shirt.

Andy gave me a nod of approval as I walked out of the bathroom, wearing black trousers and a white shirt. Just formal enough without being a full suit, I've always hated suits.

"Okay, we better go. We are already late."

We made it to the meeting room just in time, the Alpha hadn't arrived yet. Luckily for us. I couldn't help but notice every wolf staring at us as we entered the room, what the hell is their problem.

Andy shifted uncomfortably under their gaze, causing Logan to pull her closer to him. Resting an arm on her back to comfort her. The simple act made me miss my mate, the idea of having my mate in my arms sounded amazing to me. Especially right now, my wolf was on edge and honestly so am I. Something feels wrong, like a part of me is missing. Until she is mine, I won't feel whole again.

I cannot understand how Andy survived Connor's rejection; I am not ashamed to admit that my sister is stronger than me. She is the strongest person I know and has survived more pain than I would wish on anybody.

But here I sit, going crazy because I haven't seen my mate since yesterday. Strong is not the word I would use to describe myself; I have always dreamed of the day I would meet my mate. I never imagined it would go like this.

You, okay? Andy's voice rang through my head, pulling me out of my thoughts.

The door opened and in walked a man I hadn't met yet, though his commanding power made it obvious he was the alpha.

The room fell silent as he took his seat, no one dared speak before him. Even his own pack were terrified of him, who is the guy?

The only one who didn't appear fazed was Michael, he sat at the head of the table, impatiently waiting for his son. His gaze never left Andy, his hatred for her evident on his face.

"We are here to discuss the rogue situation; I have asked the blue moon pack to aid us in our fight. I am sure you have seen them around the pack house." as Erik spoke, everyone nodded.

A wolf openly scoffed at him, at their alpha. Who does he think he is? He slouched in his chair like an overconfident idiot. Glaring at Andy and Logan, not paying any attention to the enraged alpha staring at him. It was obvious that he was his beta, nobody else would dare to talk back to their alpha like that. Even a beta though should be smart enough not to do it publicly.

The thing that shocked me though was that Eric wasn't the one to reprimand him. Michael stood, using every ounce of Alpha tone as he spoke.

"How dare you act like a disrespectful child in front of your alpha. Do not think I will not teach you respect boy."

To his credit the beta didn't back down, he stood up before yelling back.

"We don't need their help, what could we possibly need them for."

Andy looked about ready to lunge for him as he pointed towards her.

Have I missed something?

Michael walks towards the beta, grabbing him.

"Sam, apologise." Eric spoke, trying to save his beta.

Sam grunted before finally sighing as he muttered

a pathetic apology.

"Now that's over, how about we get back to work." The group turned back to Eric as if nothing had happened.

What the hell is wrong with this pack?

They are all insane.

Andy's POV

Two hours, that's how long I've been listening to idiots talk. I say talk, but all they do is argue. Every attempt I have made to speak is just met with glares. And every glare is met with a growl from Logan.

A never-ending cycle.

So here I sit, trying to stay quiet and listen. At least their current solution isn't stupid. Michael suggested they set a trap, one of their warriors overheard the rogues saying they are coming back.

So, the plan is to let them in, once they think they have won, we attack.

Woman and children will evacuate to the basement of the pact house. The rest of us fighters will get the rogues when they least expect it. I'll admit, it's not perfect but with the lack of warriors here there wasn't much choice. We needed the advantage of surprise to have a chance.

"How you doing little one?"

Logan asked as we walk out of the pack house. Hours of being in that meeting made me long for fresh air. This pack land truly is beautiful.

"I'm okay, just happy to be out of there."

Pulling me into his arms, Logan leaned down bringing his lips to mine.

"Not as much as I am little one."

Wrapped in each other's arms, we continue to walk through the fairy-tale like garden.

Chapter 12

Verity's POV

I met my mate.

How is that even possible?

Why would I say yes to meeting him, it's not like I can be with him?

Why did he have to look like that?

Like something out of a god damn magazine, how is that possible fair.

How can you show me someone so amazing, who I can never be with? I almost gave into this stupid mate bond last night, I let myself talk to him. To think about the possibility but just as always. Fate reminded me of my place.

Alpha had linked me, he was furious. Apparently, Sam had told him I left the packhouse without permission.

I had to leave Alexi, if they find out about him, I'm dead. The sadness on his face made my heart ache.

The Beta's Mate

How could I be so reckless?

How could I agree to meet him, what was I thinking?

I should know better; I do know better.

Then why can't I get him out of my head. Those pale blue eyes haunted, my dreams, making me wake up with such an intense longing for him.

How is that even possible, I barely know him. How can a stranger get to me so much? Even now, as I attempt to make the packs dinner all I can think about is him. His eyes, his goofy smile.

What's happening to me?

"Verity, hurry up. We're hungry." Sam's angered voice pulled me out of my daydreaming. Right back to work.

Rushing I plate up all the food. Before taking it out, with the help of a couple omegas.

I freeze as I step into the dinner room, its filled with the pack. They're all in here already.

Even the visiting pack members are here, the strange girl smiled at me as I set her food down. The warrior next to her is definitely the alpha, he's huge. And her mate, that's obvious by the way he looks at her.

I felt eyes on my back, as I turned my eyes locked with a beautiful pair of pale blue ones.

Alexi.

The girl, Luna of the other pack reached over and put her hand on him. A growl slipped from my lips before I could stop it.

Who the hell does she think she is, to touch what isn't hers? Her eyes widened as she looked at me, before her lips spread into the biggest smile.

"Sorry, we haven't met yet. I'm Andy, Alexi's sister." She said as she reached out a hand to me.

Sister?

I felt my body relax before replying.

"Verity, it's nice to meet you."

Our introductions are cut short by the sound of growling.

Hurrying I grabbed the rest of the plates to bring out before running back to my room. Never daring to glance up from the ground again.

He's going to kill me.

If he finds out about Alexi, he'll make my life a living hell. I'm not supposed to talk to anyone let alone mate.

What am I doing?

Sitting on my bed I watched as the sun began to fall. It reached the horizon before I grabbed my jacket and ran.

I need to see him, even if I can't be with him, I just want to see him again.

The garden was deafly quiet as I arrived, for a second, I thought he wouldn't show. Maybe he's changed his mind about being mated to the pack runt. My fears began to fade as I heard him speak.

"Please show, please show."

He's not talking to me, that much is obvious. Taking a deep breath, I put him out of his misery.

"Hi."

Alexi jumped before turning to look at me, his cheeks a gorgeous shade of red.

"You came."

I had forgotten just how gorgeous his eyes are, his scruffy brown hair and piercing blue eyes have me rooted to the spot. I want to squirm and shy away from his penetrating stare, but I can't move.

In this moment, I'm a prisoner to him. I know my cheeks are flushed based on the heat flooding my body. I still can't look away; everything is drawing me to him.

Its taking all of my strength not to jump his bones. What the hell is wrong with me?

Apparently having a mate sends my inhibitions flying out the window.

Alexi shuffles on his feet, making me realise I have just been ogling him this entire time.

Goddesses kill me.

His mouth tugs up into a sexy smirk, as he reached a handout to grasp mine. The feeling of electricity spreads up my arm at the touch. I know I'm wearing the cheesiest grin as we walk towards the woods, following a tiny stone path.

We keeping walking through the darkness, I have absolutely no idea how he can see where he's going.

"Where are you taking me?"

Ignoring my question, he keeps walking.

Opening my eyes, I saw a blanket laid out with a string of lights in the trees surrounding it.

The lake stretched out behind, a pale reflection of the moon glimmering across the water.

"Do you like it?" The worry in his voice confused me.

"If you don't, we can go somewhere else." From the corner of my eye, I watched as he ran his fingers through his hair. Shuffling on his feet. He's nervous.

"It's perfect."

Before I have a chance to ask again, my stupid clumsy ass trips on one of the stones.

Closing my eyes, bracing for the impact with the floor but it never comes. Instead, I feel electricity covering my entire body, the sensation is one of the best things I've ever felt.

Alexi smiles down at me, holding me bridal style in his arms.

"Thank you." I whisper.

"No need to thank me Love. I will always catch you." His voice is low and soft, a hypnotising sound that makes me want to pull him towards me. To be closer to me.

Like he can read my thoughts, he pulls me closer to his chest. So, close I can feel his heartbeat. Our eyes lock, for a second the whole world disappears as he leans down and presses his lips to mine.

The electricity coursing through me ignites with one kiss I'm completely addicted to him.

For a moment I allowed myself to enjoy this man in front of me. For a moment I allowed myself to give in to him. For a moment I felt free. But as our lips disconnected my world came crashing down all at once.

And with it the realisation that this isn't my life, I don't get the happy ending. There is no prince charming coming to save me, as amazing as Alexi is. I'm trapped here with *him.*

My father had always told me, no runt gets a mate. He's right, this will always be my life. I accepted that years ago. I spent so long wishing for a mate, for someone to save me. The hope destroyed me more than anyone else, every time I would begin to feel safe, he would destroy it and me. I don't have enough fight left to survive that again.

Despite all of that, the smile covering Alexi's face maybe worth all of the pain in the world.

Maybe I can do this, maybe I get to be someone else.

Maybe there is hope.

That's all I see in his eyes. Hope.

Setting me on my feet he led me to the blanket. As soon as I was comfortably positioned, he sat beside me. A massive grin still covering his face as he unpacked a picnic basket I hadn't noticed.

"I wasn't sure what you'd want, so I got a bit of everything."

He wasn't kidding, the basket was filled to the brim, the smell of cookies, chocolate and cake overwhelmed me.

He passed the basket to me and motioned for me to take something. My stomach growled as I too a slice of cake.

Alexi copied me and we both sat in comfortable

silence watching the water.

"I'm sorry."

Confused I turned to him.

"For what?"

"For scary you last night."

"You didn't."

He paused, considering my answer before he continued.

"If I didn't scare you then what did?"

What do I say?

I cant tell him the truth, but I'm a horrible liar.

"Its nothing really." I said.

Trying to avoid the topic all together, though from his expression that wasn't going to happen.

"Verity, what happened?" moving to get up he stopped me, grabbing a hold of my arm.

A whimper slipped from my lips before I could stop it.

Immediately he released me.

"Are you hurt?"

Shaking my head, I tried to move away again, this time making it to my feet before he stopped me.

"Please, talk to me Love, whatever happened I will help you." His eyes bored into mine with so much honestly, I had to look away.

"I cant."

Alexis face fell, his expression hurt. Without looking at me, he pulled my sleeve up.

A growl slipped from his lips.

I didn't have to open my eyes, I knew what he would see. My arm was covered in a dark bruise that went from my shoulder down to my wrist.

"Who did this to you?" he growled.

Flinching back, I stumbled out of his grip.

His black eyes dimed to blue as he stared at me, a guilty expression on his face.

"I'm sorry Love."

Where are you? Alpha's voice rang threw my head like a foghorn. I could feel his anger seeping through his words.

I'm frozen, my whole body is shaking as Alexi moves towards me. Confusion covering his face.

"Are you okay Love?"

I know you can hear me, so hear this. If you are not in my office in five minutes. I will kill that boy with you.

No, no. he can't.

Running, ignoring Alexi's protests. I have to get back. The packhouse is almost two miles, I'm not going to make it.

I know Alexi is going to hate me, but I won't let them hurt him. Running straight through the door and up the stairs, not paying any attention to the stares from the pack members as I ran.

The first person I see as I enter his office is the alpha, sitting on his makeshift throne. A massive wooden chair with a wolfs head carved into it.

My heart is pounding so loud in my ears as I force myself to look at him.

He smiles at me, enjoying my pain, Alexi's pained face crosses my mind. He did that. He took my happiness from me. He will always take my happiness from me.

Anger makes my bones feel like they are shaking as u see nothing but red. I refuse to cower in front of this man, the alpha who forces his will and beats anyone not willing to obey his rules.

I never will again, no matter what he does to me. I can handle pain; I can handle his attempts to break me.

"You will not disobey me girl, did you really think I wouldn't find out you're screwing their beta." A growl slips from his lips as he walks over to me, grabbing my throat as I squirm to break free.

"I told you, you're mine. I own you girl, do not forget that." He seethed before throwing me against the wall.

Before I can get up, he hits me again. Hard. The taste of blood fills my mouth.

I will not break.

Grabbing my head, his fingers dig into my scalp as he lifts me until I'm dangling on the tips of my toes. He slams his hand into my ribs, and I wince. The pain ripples across my chest.

I will not break.

"You think you're being tough? You think that he

will save you?" he asked, humour in his voice.

"You are nothing, a runt. When he figures that out, he will want nothing to do with you." He growled, before throwing me to the ground.

"If you even try to see him again, I will kill him. And that my dear, is a promise."

I watched as he left the room before hugging my knees to my chest as sobs wracked my entire body.

"Verity, are you okay?" Molly's voice stuttered, fear making her shake.

I hadn't even heard her come in, when did she get here?

She jumped back in shock as I lifted my face to hers, only now seeing my bloody face. Tears welled in her eyes as she knelt in front of me, reaching her hand out she traced the cuts and bruises on my face.

"Let's get you cleaned up." She whispered, reaching for my arm to help me stand. Slowly we made our way back to my room, luckily the hallways were empty.

"You don't have to help me." I said as I sat on my bed. The smallest smile graced her lips before she spoke.

"I Want to, don't worry about me. Sam is on patrol all night."

I had forgotten how much I missed her; she was my best friend. My only friend. Before she met Sam, we were so close.

"Thank you."

She smiled again, brighter this time before walking into the bathroom. Returning moments later, a bowl of water and cloth in her hands. Trying my best to stay still as she wiped and dabbed at every cut, my body still involuntarily winced away.

"I can't believe he did this to you." She sobbed, tears welling in her eyes again.

Speechless I just stared at her, what's so shocking about this. This is what he was like, what he had always been like.

"Why?"

For a moment she stared at me, searching my face for answers. I could see guilt flooding her eyes until eventually she had to look away.

"I... I always knew he was mean but... I... I never knew he was so cruel." She stammered. Her voice shaking with every word.

Had she not known? I had spent so long furious with her, for leaving me alone. Do any of them know? They all avoid me, never treating me as a part of the pack. But did they know the whole story? I had always thought everybody knew, knew who he truly was.

"I swear, if I had known."

"It's okay Molly, there's nothing you could have done."

Shaking her head, her eyes focused on mine again.

"If I was anything like that girl, the one who saved us. I could have done something."

"Andy."

Molly raised her eyebrow at me, confusion covering her features.

"The girl, her name's Andy, she's the packs Luna."

"From the way she handled Sam, I thought she was an Alpha."

Molly was right, I thought the same. Until Alexi told me different.

"How do you know her?"

Avoiding her questioning gaze, I stared at my hands, chewing on the side of my lip.

"You're not telling me something V, you always bite your lip when you're lying."

"I don't know her, but I do know her brother."

Molly crossed her arms, eyebrow still raised. Waiting for me to continue.

"He's, my mate." I whispered.

I could practically hear her mind blowing up, the room fell into a deafening silence as I waited for her to reply.

"You have a mate?" she exclaimed, jumping off of the bed.

"What's his name? is he cute?"

Just like that she was back to the same old Molly, a kind-hearted girl who never stopped talking.

"He's, He's perfect. But it doesn't matter."

Molly sat beside me, holding my hand in hers.

"What do you mean it doesn't matter? You get to leave; you can be with him away from this place."

"No, I can't."

"Why the hell not V? You deserve to be happy; you deserve to be free of that monster."

"Because he will kill him. I know he will, if I even talk to Alexi again, he will kill him." I said before my best friend, and I leaned into each other as tears overwhelmed me.

Chapter 13

Alexi's POV

As I stared at the forest in front of me, I felt frozen.

She left, again.

This was all my fault, why did I get so mas at her. I hadn't meant to, I just couldn't stop myself. Someone had hurt her.

It feels as if my heart is aching in my chest, a wave of emptiness is sweeping over me.

Despite my hesitation, I make my way back to the packhouse.

There is so much I wish I knew, so I could figure out what I was doing wrong, and why she is so against us.

Andy will know what to do, she always knows what to do.

I heard Andy and Logan before I even reached their door.

"Logan, stop!" Andy yelled giggling.

"Make me, Little one."

After sighing, I leave and go back to my room. It's unfair for me to put my problems on Andy.

My thoughts drifted to my mate as I collapsed on my bed. How did I get here? Three times in twenty-four hours since I met my mate, she has run away from me. Where am I going wrong? Did I say the wrong thing, did I do the wrong thing?

Kissing her had been the best moment of my life. The feeling of holding her close, of having her so close, was addicting. She was out of my arms in an instant, and I suddenly felt empty, as if a part of me had been taken away.

My thoughts stayed on my mate until eventually I drifted into an uncomfortable sleep.

"Alexi, wake up!"

Andy's voice echoed through my room waking me up. Groaning I opened the door, only to be met with Andy's annoyed face.

"What's up little sister?"

"What's up? Are you kidding, I've been trying to mind link you all morning! Why did you block me? I've been worried sick!" she all but yelled at me.

"I didn't block you, I blocked everyone. Sorry, I didn't mean to worry you."

Her face softened before she spoke. "What happened? Did the date not go well?"

Sighing I collapsed on my bed, Andy following my lead. Avoiding her scrutinising gaze, I kept head on the pillows as I recounted last night. Andy stayed quiet the entire time, listening to every word. The more I talked the sadder her expression became, until she had tears in her eyes.

"Oh Lex, I'm sorry. Maybe... Maybe it's not what you think, I mean there could be another reason she ran."

I know she's trying to make me feel better but it's not working, I don't think anything will ever get rid of this empty feeling. I've never felt so incomplete.

"Again." I snapped, unable to stop myself.

"What?"

"She ran *again*. What other reason could there be? She's running from me."

Andy's arms wrapped around me, holding me impossibly close. A sense of déjà vu fell over me, the memory of holding Andy's crying form after the rejection with Connor. The thought of rejection made my stomach plummet, a boulder-sized pit of dread forming in my gut.

Is she going to reject me?

My wolf howled in my head; he was going to lose her without ever really meeting her.

Andy squeezed my hand and gave me a reassuring smile before standing up. Her hand reached out and pulled me to my feet.

"We are getting out of here, staying in this room all day is not going to do you any good."

It had taken some convincing, but Andy had managed to get me out of the pack house. Dragging me through the trees, until we came to a pond. I have to admit it was beautiful. The sun shone down and reflected off of the still water, making it resemble an oil painting.

"How did you know this was here?" I asked.

"Technically Logan found it, its amazing right? Like something out of a fairy-tale."

Splashing in the water drew my attention, a child no more than eight was playing in the water. Of everything at Silvercrest this was the only thing that had felt like a normal pack. A kid playing in the water on a hot day. When he noticed us, his smile widened, and he waved at Andy.

"Hey Tom." She yelled.

I stared at my sister confused but she just shrugged her shoulders before giggling to herself. A look of mischief on her face. Before I could react, she pushed me towards the water. With a massive splash I crashed into the pond.

"You're so dead." I growled as I waded through the water towards my giggling sister.

She squealed as I picked her up and threw her in, before jumping in and joining her. Tom was watching us laughing, enjoying the show.

For a while I forgot about everything and just enjoyed having my sister to myself. Selfish or not, I needed her after the past few days.

My thoughts drifted to Verity again, and before I knew it the emptiness returned.

A thunderous growl snapped me back to the present as Andy lunged for the kid, knocking him down under the water.

What the hell?

Within seconds a wolf leaped from the woods, landing in front of them. Teeth snapping, as he growled at them. The water only coming up to his neck.

Rogue. Andy linked.

The wolf jumped towards them again, claws raised. Andy shielded Tom, leaving her back exposed. The wolfs claws ripped at her shoulder, turning the water around her crimson.

Anger pulsed through my veins a I charged for the wolf, my body colliding with his, sending us both flying. Without pausing I grabbed the wolf by the neck, easily snapping it. His body went limp in my arms, throwing him to the ground I went to my sister.

She was still standing in the water, her arms

swaying slightly. Scooping her up I ran towards the pack house, the sound of Tom's footsteps echoed through the woods as he struggled to keep up.

Bursting through the doors a group of omegas gawked at us, before seeing Andy's bloody shirt and pointing towards a door on the far side of the entrance. Relief flooded through me as we entered the pack hospital, it was smaller than ours, only one doctor and a few nurses.

"What happened?" the doctor asked as he studied her wounds.

"A rogue jumped us."

He nodded before ushering me out of the room, away from my sister.

Andy was attacked by a rouge. I linked Logan.

What! The growl in his voice sent a chill down my spine.

She's getting checked out, the doctors with her now.

A minute passed and I thought maybe he hadn't heard me.

Is she okay?

I could hear the doctor talking to Andy, a cut nothing serious.

She's going to be fine, a couple of stitches.

Relief flooded through the link.

Do me a favour Lex?

Of course.

Keep her busy, I need a couple of hours. Just until the sun's gone down.

A nurse walked over to me, a smile on her face as she bowed to me.

The doctors finished now; I will try to distract her.

Thank you.

"You can see her now."

Without hesitating I rushed into the room, uttering a thank you. Andy was sitting on the exam table, a massive smile etched on her face.

I hesitated, staring at her. "Are you okay?"

"I'm perfect, it was just a scratch Lex. A few stitches and I'm good as new."

"Really? There was so much blood."

"That's what happens when you bleed in water, come on let's go find Logan. Before he freaks out."

This maybe harder than I thought.

Chapter 14

Andy's POV

"What happened?" A doctor asked as he poked at my back.

"A rogue jumped us."

He nodded before ushering Alexi out of the room, his eyes never leaving my wound.

"Jen, take some blood. We need to make sure the rogue wasn't diseased."

A short woman appeared out of nowhere sticking a needle into my arm, wincing I groaned.

"Are you hurt anywhere else, other than your back?"

I shook my head, and he went back to work.

"You're going to need stitches, but you will be fine."

While the doctor started his work, I relaxed on the table sighing with relief. After he finished, he left me alone to rest.

I was woken when the door opened, and the doctor walked toward me with an apology in his eyes.

"I'm sorry I didn't realise you were sleeping."

"It's okay, I didn't either."

"I was able to get the results back and the rogue was clean. Something came up in your tests, so I ran another one." He handed me the piece of paper in his hands, confused when I began to read it.

"I wasn't sure if you knew." Shaking my head, I stared at the results, too shocked to form words. It read in large, bold letters.

Result of pregnancy: Positive.

Oh. My. Goddess.

I know I should be terrified, I'm eighteen! But in this moment, all I feel is a sense of overwhelming joy. The thought of a mini-Logan running around, all chubby cheeked and adorable is enough to dwell the panic building inside of me.

My wolf howled in joy.

I take it you're excited.

A pup!!! We're having a pup!!!

I couldn't help but agree with her, we're having a pup!

Logan, I need to tell Logan.

"Thank you, can I go home now." I pleaded with the doctor.

He smiled at me before nodding, "Let me send in your friend and then you can leave."

A few minutes later Alexi walked in the room, hesitating at the door.

"Are you okay?"

"I'm perfect, it was just a scratch Lex. A few stitches and I'm good as new."

"Really? There was so much blood."

"That's what happens when you bleed in water, come on let's go find Logan. Before he freaks out."

I need to find my mate.

Scrunching the paper in my pocket I jump off the

table and we head upstairs.

Where is he, we've searched the whole packhouse and Logan is nowhere to be seen. My excitement is beginning to turn to anxiety. Where is my mate!

No-one has seen or heard from him all day, even Alexi hasn't heard anything. Every time I try to link him, I'm just met with silence.

"Where is he?"

Alexi palmed the back of his neck, shifting slightly.

"Alexi! If you know where he is, you better tell me."

Hello Little one. Logan's voice echoed in my mind.

Relief flooded me, making my heart beat slow.

Where have you been??? I yelled throw the link.

I could hear the guilt in his voice.

I'm sorry Little one.

Where were you?

Silence...

Meet me outside.

Why?

Again silence.

Do you trust me?

Without hesitation I replied *Always.*

I could practically see the goofy grin on his face.

Trusting my mate I went outside, leaving Alexi smiling in the bedroom.

The second I stepped outside of the packhouse two massive arms engulfed me as the scent of chocolate filled my nose.

"Hello Little one."

Before I could turn to face my mate, he lifted me up in his arms, holding me bridal style.

"Logan, what are you doing?"

He grinned down at me, "Its a surprise, close your eyes. And keep them closed until I tell you."

Without a second thought I closed my eyes and let my mate lead me.

"Where are you taking me handsome?"

Silence.

He didn't say anything just kept leading me through the trees. It was obvious we were heading to the forest because I kept tripping over the roots of the trees.

"Okay, stay right there and don't open your eyes until I tell you."

Nodding, I waited patiently, listening to the running water of a stream nearby. After a few minutes of waiting, I started to feel nervous again.

"Logan?"

Silence.

A feeling of unease flooded through me.

Logan?

Again, nothing but silence.

Before I could open my eyes, I felt a hit to the back of my head before my world went black.

Chapter 15

Verity's POV

I know what I have to do.

I have to reject him.

Even thinking the words sends a chill to my heart, I don't know if I can do this. I just know I have to. To protect him, to keep him safe I have to let him go.

I can't let him die, I won't.

After just a few days he already means everything to me, and I am already willing to give up everything for him.

What if Molly's right? What if I could run away with him?

Sighing I collapsed on the bed, there is no way he would let me leave here. I have to reject Alexi, it's the only way to make sure he doesn't get dragged into my life.

I need to find him before I talk myself out of this.

Checking my makeup one last time, making sure every bruise is covered and unnoticeable I walk out of my room to find my mate.

Goddess forgive me.

The packhouse was almost empty, lunch had finished, and everyone was going about the rest of their day.

When I couldn't find him inside, I thought maybe he had left, until I saw him sitting in the garden.

His face was etched in such a sad expression it took everything in me not to comfort him. I have brought him nothing but pain, and now I'm going to give him more.

How is it fair he looks like that? How can someone be so handsome, sexy and cute at the same time.

He straightened in his seat as I approached him. The hope in his eyes as they met mine was crippling.

"Verity, are you okay?"

Everything I had planned to say vanished from my mind, leaving me lost for words.

My voice came out barely above a whisper. "I, I'm

sorry for running."

His face softens as he reached an arm out to me.

"You don't have to apologise, but if something is wrong you can tell me Love. I promise I will do everything I can to help you."

The honesty in his voice broke my heart, I couldn't stop the tears in my eyes from falling as I began to sob.

His arms wrapped around me as he lifted me into his lap, resting my head on his chest I allowed myself to find comfort in him.

Placing soft kisses on my forehead he whispered to me.

"Shhs it's okay, you're okay. I promise you; I will keep you safe Love."

I do not deserve this man; I will never deserve this man. I'm nothing, I'm not even a wolf. How can I have been paired with him? He's a beta! I'm not even considered good enough to be an Omega.

We stayed like that for the longest time, just taking comfort in each other. His hands traced my back until they touch one of my bruises and I involuntarily winced.

His chest shook as a growl slipped from his lips.

"Are you hurt?"

I shook my head but before I could respond the sound of an alarm interrupted our conversation. Alexi jumped up, placing me firmly on my feet.

"The rogues, they must be back. Go into the packhouse, hide."

I grabbed his arm, holding him back.

"Don't go please."

I could see the conflict in his eyes as he bent down and placed a soft kiss on my forehead.

"I'll be back Love, I promise." He whispered before running towards the blaring alarm.

A sense of emptiness filled me and for a brief second, I understood the pain I had put Alexi through by running. Listening to my mate I ran towards the packhouse, swerving around the warriors heading towards the fight.

"Verity." Molly's voice pulled my attention, she was running towards me dodging between the crowd. As soon as she was within reach, I grabbed her hand, keeping it firmly in mine as we made our way downstairs.

"I've never seen it so crazy, even for rogues."

"I think something else is going on." She whispered as we sat in the far corner of the basement. She must have seen my confused expression because she carried on explaining, keeping an eye on the wolves around us.

"Sam and the Alpha had a meeting about the rogue attack."

"That doesn't sound very suspicious Mol, Sam is the head warrior."

"Two weeks ago, they had the meeting two weeks ago."

"How is that even possible? The attack was only a few days ago? Maybe Sam told you the wrong date?"

She shook her head, an exasperated sigh leaving her mouth.

"He didn't tell me, I overheard the meeting, to be honest I think he forgets I exist sometimes."

Fear flooded me, choking me.

"What is it?" she whispered.

"Alexi, Bluemoon came to help us with the rogues. If the Alpha knew, then why would he call them? He never asks for help; he hates other packs."

Molly's face paled as I spoke.

"Sam said something yesterday that didn't make sense to me."

A small growl left my lips, causing a few wolves to glance at us. Molly's voice lowered to a whisper.

"He said 'they've bought every word of it'."

My legs started moving and I ran towards the door ignoring Molly's panicked cries.

Please be wrong…

Please be wrong…

He wouldn't.

As soon as I reached the trees, I had my answer.

Silence.

No fighting, no rogues, no warriors protecting the packhouse.

What am I doing?

I'm not a fighter, if they catch me, I'm dead.

The words please be okay are running through my head on a loop, a silent prayer to the goddess.

"Alpha, we have managed to secure them in the cells."

I froze, hiding behind the trees.

"Did they suspect anything?"

"No Sir. They never got the chance. The Luna is still unconscious however, the male was harder to takedown, he's pretty banged up."

There was a pause before he replied.

"Send in an omega to clean him up, I want to speak with him."

After the Alpha left, I walked towards the warrior, please work!

My plan worked perfectly, within a few seconds the warrior called to me.

"You, go down to cell one, prisoners wounded."

Thank you, Goddess!

"Yes Sir."

"Be quick about it, Alpha wants to talk to him."

Keeping my eyes down I run into the bathroom grabbing the first aid kit and a wet cloth. The walk down to the cells felt agonisingly long, every step echoing in the small space.

A guard stood at the door watching me approach. Keeping my head low, I spoke.

"Alpha sent me for the wounded prisoner."

He moved, opening the doors for me.

"Last one down the left."

As I walked down the hallway, I felt myself calming.

I can't believe that worked!

Either I'm great at this or they're awful at it. I would bet on the later.

What I saw when I entered the room almost brought me to my knees. Alexi was huddled in the corner, wrists bound. Deep gashes covered his arms and back. A growl slipped from his lips as I got closer to him. Ignoring the warning I reached down and ran my hand along his shoulder, being careful to avoid his wounds. Sparks danced across my fingertips at the contact.

Alexi's head snapped up, his eyes widening as they met mine.

"Verity?"

I smiled at him as I wiped his cuts with the cloth.

"What are you doing here? It's not safe."

"They sent me down to clean you up."

He stayed quiet, patient as I checked every wound.

"You're good at this." He mumbled, obviously trying to lighten the mood.

"I've had a lot of practice."

The words slipped from my mouth before I could stop them. Alexi stared down at me, his face filled with questions.

"I'm sorry."

"For what Love?"

"I should have known it was a trap."

He gripped my hand in his, pulling me closer.

"This is not your fault."

"Yes, it is, him calling you should have been obvious. He hates guests even before he never allowed anyone on our lands."

Alexi paused, thinking through his answer before speaking.

"This isn't your fault, I'm the one who decided to come here. Besides this has all led me to you."

His fingers traced my lips, and I took a step back- out of reach. A pained expression crossed his face.

"I'm sorry, I swear it's not what you think. It's just I can't risk them seeing." I motioned to the door, and he nodded, his expression softening.

"I understand Love, do you know where Andy and Logan are?"

"She's in another cell unconscious, I haven't heard anything about him. I'm sorry."

A growl slipped from his lips.

"I need you to do something for me."

I answered him without hesitation.

"Anything."

A smirk covered his face before he continued.

Chapter 16

Andy's POV

Where am I?

The room was poorly lit and made it almost impossible to see anything. As I tried to stand, I realised my hands were tied together. What the hell is happening to me?

My wolf felt distant, so far, I couldn't reach her.

Wolfsbane.

My hands instinctively reached for my belly.

Please be okay.

"I promise little one, I will get us out of here."

We just need to find your father.

Mind linking him wasn't working, silently I sent a prayer to the moon goddess that the wolfsbane wouldn't harm the pup.

My thoughts were cut short by my whole body freezing as every nerve felt exposed.

The sound of pained howling filled the room.

It's not my pain.

Logan!

I'll kill them.

My body rushes to the bars, gripping them in my hands ignoring the burning sensation as I try to break my way out.

"It's no use."

Why is this happening?

One minute I'm talking to my mate, the next I wake up in a cage.

How the hell have I been kidnapped twice!

Another pained howl echo's through the walls.

"Logan I'm here."

The second I get out of here I will kill every one of them.

Curling into a ball, I cried as my mates pained howls filled my head.

Verity's POV

"Are you sure this is a good idea?" Molly asked for the twentieth time. As we unlocked the door to Alexi's room.

Rolling my eyes, I walk into the room molly following me closely muttering to herself.

"Why did I agree to this?"

"You didn't. I never asked you to come with me."

She scoffed at me.

"Yeah, because I'm going to let you do this on your own."

I couldn't stop smiling at my *friend*.

It had been so long since I could call anyone that.

"Did he say where it would be?"

I shook my head, pulling out the draws.

Nothing, where would a guy leave their phone?

"Got it!" Molly yelled triumphantly.

"It was in the cupboard."

She must have noticed my confused expression.

"Men are weird." She said shrugging, her shoulders.

Molly passed me the phone, before I even got a look at it, the sound of the door had us both turning.

Molly's face paled as we watched the door handle rattle.

What are we going to do? Molly Linked.

Hide.

We both rushed to lay flat under the bed.

This is not going to work. Molly hissed through the link.

The door opened, footsteps moving straight to us.

We watched as he makes his way to the bedside table, ignoring the bed.

Papers fly everywhere as he shuffles through the pile.

One of the pieces catches my eye as it lays flat on the ground.

A drawing, of a grey wolf with blue eyes staring through the trees. A dirt-coloured border surrounding it. Making the paper crumple at the sides.

I remember that picture, I drew it years ago.

It had always been one of my favourites.

I must have dropped it by the lake, the day I met Alexi.

He kept it.

A warm feeling spread through my chest; the feeling evaporated as soon as the intruder spoke.

"I know you're in here somewhere."

Sam! Molly's fear came through the link in waves. Her hand gripped mine so tight I was sure she would break it.

What do we do?

Stay quiet?

But he knows we are in here.

I squeezed her hand offering the only comfort I could in the moment.

Trust me.

We both stay silent as Sam makes his way around the room looking through everything, his anger building the longer he looks. Eventually after what feels like hours he stops. Sighs frustrated and leaves the room.

We both stay silent for a breath before getting out from under the bed.

Molly stars babbling as her adrenaline fades. Ignoring her I go straight to my drawing holding it close.

"Hello? V? are you even listening to me?"

"Sorry Mol, I didn't hear a word."

Rolling her eyes at me she repeated herself.

"I said, how did you know he wasn't talking to us?"

"That's easy, he sounded annoyed."

Molly raised her eyebrows at me confused.

"If he was talking to us, he would have sounded furious. He hates me remember."

"It's not just you he hates." Molly's voice was so low I almost didn't hear her.

I felt angry for my friend, how could she have been mated to that monster. She always talked about finding her mate, even when we were kids, she was so excited.

How could such a sweet and kind person be so unlucky.

"Come on V, lets get out of here, I don't want him to come back." Molly said walking towards the door.

"Did he tell you who to call?"

"Someone named Grayson."

Chapter 17

Verity's POV

Getting into Andy's cell was a lot easier than I had thought.

There were less guards than Alexi's cell and an omega carrying a tray of food for a prisoner didn't raise any alarms.

As soon as I reached the door, I could hear her crying. Entering the room, I saw Andy huddled on the bed, head in her hands as her sobs shook her whole body.

My heart ached for this girl I barely knew.

"Andy?"

Her head shot up, she stood and walked towards me.

"Verity? What are you doing down here?"

"Alexi sent me."

She smiled, pulling me towards the bed.

"Tell me everything."

After I had told Andy everything that had happened since they where taken, we just sat there in silence as she took it all in. eventually Andy broke the silence.

"So, Grayson's coming?"

"Yes, he said he'll be here as soon as he can, well technically he said, 'not again'."

Andy chuckled at my words.

"I may have been kidnapped before."

I just stared at her as she shrugged her shoulders.

"It happens, so what's the plan V?"

My eyes shot to hers.

I still couldn't understand how they can all accept me so easily.

"We need to lower you dose of wolfsbane so you can shift and escape."

"Slight problem with that."

"What's the problem?"

"I can't shift."

My heart stopped, is she like me?

She can't be a runt.

"I'm pregnant."

Why would Alexi want a pregnant she wolf to turn?

Pregnant wolves can't shift, it's too risky for the pup.

"Why would he want you to shift?"

"Because he doesn't know, no one does. I only found out this morning."

"I'm not sure what we are going to do, the plan was for you to shift and break the bars to get out."

Andy smiled at me.

"It's a good thing I don't need to shift to break the bars."

"I don't understand."

"It's a long story, I just need to get these cuffs off. They're covered in wolfsbane"

I can't believe this is going to work, Alexi's plan is going to work. A sense of relief flooded through me; my mate is going to be okay.

I have been so focused on helping him I hadn't taken the time to really consider the danger my mate has been in.

My mate.

I was so certain of my choice this morning but after seeing Alexi in pain, the thought of losing him is unbearable.

Alexi is my mate.

And as terrifying as it may be, I'm not going to reject him.

I can't I don't care what happens to me, I will not reject him.

For the first time in forever I feel happy, I feel like I have found my home.

For the first time in my life, I feel excited.

I don't make it out of the basement before someone grips my arm, pulling me back.

As if the universe is proving me wrong.

"Do you honestly think I'm stupid?"

Before I can react, I feel myself colliding with the walls of the tunnel.

"You think I wouldn't find out you went to see their beta again?"

Frozen, all I feel is numb. I can't move I can't breathe.

"I told you what would happen, if you saw him again."

"No."

"What did you just say to me girl?" he growled out grabbing me by my hair he pulled me into one of the rooms.

"Bring the others, lets teach her just how true to my word I am." He yelled towards a warrior I hadn't noticed was here.

No... please no...

"All of them Alpha?"

"Yes, lets get this mess over with."

No, Goddess please no.

He grabbed me again, pulling me towards the wall. Throwing me on the floor.

It didn't take long for one of the warriors to come in Alexi trailing behind.

Alexi stiffened as his eyes connected with mine.

I had failed, after everything we did, it wouldn't matter.

I was going to die.

Alexi was going to die, because of me.

What have I done?

Alexi struggled against his restraints, but it was no use, there's too much wolfsbane in his system. He couldn't fight back, and he knew it.

The pain in his eyes betrayed him, he was scared and afraid.

"I'm sorry." I whispered as they pushed him to kneel beside me.

Alexi looked towards me confused.

"This is not your fault Love; I shouldn't have asked you to put yourself in danger.

"You're wrong." I whispered.

Our conversation was cut short by the sound of growling as a warrior brought Logan in and forced him beside Alexi.

"Take your hands off of me" He growled at the warriors.

Logan took one look at Alexi and me and growled again.

"Where is she? If you have hurt a hair on her head, I swear on the moon Goddess herself I will kill you."

His yelling subsided as another warrior walked in, pulling a reluctant Andy behind him.

As soon as her eyes landed on Logan she stopped struggling and went to her mate. She almost made it before the warrior pulled her back. Her growl instantly made Alpha smile.

He's enjoying this.

"Now that everyone's here we can get started."

Alexi stared at him something was annoying him, I could tell. Even in this moment, as we all wait to die something is annoying him.

"Why bring us here?" Alexi asked.

"Now that is a long story."

Chapter 18

Connor's POV

My plan had worked perfectly, they did exactly what I had wanted. They had gone to Silvercrest.

Tyler had paid off a guard to disappear for a few hours, she had told him it was so we could be alone, and the idiot believed her easily. All that was left was to get out of this cell.

"Connor?"

"Did you get the key?"

"Of course."

"Good, let me out."

Tyler looked at me, playing with the key as she eyed me.

"What?"

"Promise me."

"What?"

"Promise me that I'm your mate, that you choose me."

Does she actually think I would choose her? If there's one good thing to being stuck on wolfsbane for months, it's the clarity.

I have a mate, and I will get her back from Logan.

She will be mine again.

But that isn't going to happen if I'm stuck in here.

So, for my mate and my freedom I played my part.

"Of course, baby, why would I possibly want anyone else?"

She visibly softened, a smirk covering her face.

"I knew it, I just had to be sure Connie."

With great effort I kept the smile on my face, waiting for her to unlock the door.

I watched as Tyler walked away leaving the cell door ajar before leading the guard upstairs, away from the cells.

As soon as they were out of sight, I made my move. Keeping to the shadows of the walls I made my way through the tunnels. The packhouse seemed eerily quiet as I left the basement. Ignoring it I headed for the door until I heard voices and sprinted into one of the unoccupied rooms.

"What do you mean they locked them up?"

Damon?

Another voice joined his, sounding equally pissed off.

"I mean exactly what I said, she told me it was a trap. The alphas going to kill them."

Silence.

Kill them? Does he mean Silvercrest?

No.

He was supposed to distract them.

Not kill her.

"She who? How do you know she's telling the truth?"

"I don't, but I cant reach any of them."

No.

This is all wrong.

How dare he hurt her.

They didn't know I was here and were distracted. I should escape.

I should run.

But I can't leave her.

I won't let her die.

She is never going to be hurt because of me again.

She is mine. I thought as I stepped into the open, with two pissed off wolves staring at me.

Chapter 19

Alexi's POV

"Now that is a long story." Michael was smiling, enjoying the pain he was putting us through.

The sick bastard is enjoying this.

If he so much as looks at Verity, I'll kill him.

"Then why don't you tell us." Logan growled beside me.

Michael turned his gaze showing nothing but arrogance.

Michael glared at him, before moving to stand in front of us as if he were preparing to give a speech.

"The truth is, I was told to. Normally I wouldn't have agreed with a complete stranger, however it did pique my curiosity. And when you arrived, I realised just who you were." Michael stared at me.

"I'm not anyone."

He smiled. "No, you are not, it was not you I was referring to."

He turned his gaze on Andy.

"You're a Hale, the daughter of the alpha of crescent moon. You should be long dead girl. I don't know how you survived but I promise you, you won't survive this time."

Andy stiffened.

"Why the hell do you care?" Logan growled, standing up for his mate.

"They wouldn't listen to me, I tried but it was hopeless. The alpha was an idiot."

Andy growled; the sound echoed off the walls.

"We have rules, laws. He was ignoring them. I warned him."

"What did you do?"

"I solved it, one call to a hunter and the problem was solved."

Andy's rage started building her growls filling the room.

I was sure if it weren't for the wolfsbane she would be completely engulfed in flames. Once she had started to calm, she turned on the amused alpha.

"Why? You owe me that much."

Michael smirked at her before responding.

"You my dear, your foolish father had decided to

name his daughter Alpha."

After a pause he kept talking.

"He wouldn't listen, so I had to put an end to it."

"Why." Andy whispered; her voice filled with pain.

"We have rules, he had no right to decide otherwise. His arrogance is what got him killed. All I did was call a hunter and give them an address; they did the rest."

Sick bastard.

Verity froze beside me, something he said affecting her.

I tried to get closer to her, to do something but the chains were too tight.

"I will kill you." Andy whispered her voice void of emotion.

Her face was pale, eyes cold as she stared at the alpha.

If looks could kill.

"You were always evil." Verity's voice was quite, she wasn't looking at any of us. She was talking to herself.

From the corner of my eye, I saw Michael walk towards her. He looked straight at her, in a flash I watched as his fist connected with her chest.

Verity doubled over, coughing as she tried to catch her breath.

"Touch her again and I will rip you piece from piece." I growled out.

My anger was building, everything felt wrong. There was anger but no strength behind it. The chains still stayed even as I struggled.

Without my wolf I might as well be human, useless.

My mate was in pain and all I could do was watch.

"Good luck with that boy, perhaps you should learn to keep it in your pants."

A growl slipped through my teeth.

"Stick to your own omegas and leave mine alone."

"Leave him alone." Verity's voice pulled our attention, Michael's face filled with so much contempt it baffled me. How could he hate her so much?

What could she have possibly done?

"How dare you speak to me like that."

Verity looked at him, her eyes looked on his. She was afraid but still standing up to him.

My mate is strong.

A sense of pride filled me as I watched my mate stand up to her alpha.

"I thought her death made you cruel, but you were always evil. No good person could kill a whole pack and smile at the memory."

Michael rushed for her; fist raised again.

A growl slipped past my lips stopping him in his tracks.

He looked at me, confusion covering his eyes.

Verity didn't stop though her anger only building.

"You're a monster." She shouted, her voice almost turning into a growl.

Michaels face twisted into a look of pure rage.

"You will not speak of her; you have no right."

A look of hurt filled Verity's eyes before she shouted at the angry Alpha.

"She was my mother."

Chapter 20

Verity's POV

"She was my mother."

I couldn't stop myself; I was just so angry.

He threatened my mate, he's the reason a whole pack died.

It's his fault, it's all his fault.

"And she was my mate" he growled back, his anger pouring out of him in waves. I have never seen him so angry, maybe this wasn't a good idea. If we can keep him talking long enough maybe Blue Moon will get here in time, goddess please let them get here in time.

Alexi was staring at us, his eyes wide, mouth hung open.

"He's your father?" Alexi whispered, still staring wide eyed.

"I am not her *father*, if it were up to me, we never would have had her."

I expected to feel hurt, pain, anything. But I've heard it all before.

"She's right, you are a monster. She's your daughter, how can you treat her like this?"

"She is not my daughter; she is the reason my mate is dead. Because she wouldn't listen."

Listen?

Who wouldn't listen?

"My mother wanted me?"

It wasn't until they all looked at me that I realised I had spoke out loud.

"She was delusional, it didn't matter that you were weak or broken, she held onto you. Refused to let me do what needed to be done."

"Held onto me? You told me she died in childbirth."

He looked at me, his eyes filled with anger and pain.

"I did what I had to do, but she got in the way. It was supposed to be you, you're the reason she is dead."

Numb, all I feel is numb. I didn't kill my mother, I never killed her.

All this time I thought I had killed her, how could he let me believe it was my fault?

The sound of growling pulled out attention.

Erik was standing in the doorway, his eyes pitch black as his enraged growls filled the room.

"You killed her?"

Erik was shaking as his muscles tensed, his wolf trying to break free.

I have seen my brother angry but never anything like this. He was struggling to control his wolf.

"Control your wolf son."

Michaels voice gave away no fear, the enraged alpha merely annoyed him.

"You told me Verity killed her."

Erik's words became incoherent as they turned to growls.

Within a moment Erik lunged for our father.

Knocking him to the ground, sinking his teeth into his shoulder.

Alpha howled in pain as Erik's claws sunk into his chest.

He hadn't completely turned, only his fangs and claws showing.

"You're just a coward, blaming Verity for your mistake. How could you do that to your daughter? How could you do that to me? To let me hate my own sister?" Erik growled; his words seethed with anger.

Not once have I ever heard Erik call me his sister, in eighteen years.

He took everything from us, our mother, our relationship. Because of him I have spent my whole life alone, feeling guilty for being born.

In a blink of an eye Alpha had grabbed Erik and thrown him against the wall.

"Control your wolf or I will do it for you."

Alpha growled at Erik, leaving him crumpled in a heap on the floor.

"Leave him alone." Alpha turned to me; his eyes filled with such hatred I lost my words.

"You need to remember your place girl." A smirk covered his face as he walked towards me.

"Allow me to remind you."

Alexi growled, stopping him in his tracks.

He stared at Alexi as he struggled against the chains.

"That's not possible." He whispered, more to himself than any of us.

His eyes shifted between Alexi and me as

everything clicked into place.

"He's your mate, how?"

"I have no idea." I whispered; Alexi's eyes were on me. Begging me to look at him, to explain.

"It doesn't really matter; the ending will be the same. You should have listened to me when I told you to stay away from him, mate or not."

Alexi stared at me, his eyes wide. His mind going crazy trying to figure out what was happening. His eyes never left mine, they glued to mine as if his life depended on it. Begging for answers.

He came over to me, grabbing my hair pulling me across the room. My hands weren't tied like the others, but trying as I might I was no match for my father. I am a runt, weak and helpless.

Alexi growled impossibly loud as Michael threw me into the corner, the other alpha, Logan joining in. Both trying to break out of their chains.

It was Andy however who caught my attention, she wasn't growling or fighting against the chains. Her eyes were tightly closed, her hands in fists as she knelt on the floor. Ignoring everything around her, if I hadn't seen her take on Sam without any fear, I would have thought she was trying to avoid witnessing our deaths. But she was fearless, so what is she doing. For some reason, the strangeness of it was filling my mind, making me ignore everything in the room and focus on her.

So, I was the first to see it, to see her change. Her eyes opened wide; a smirk covered her face as she stood. Her chains falling off of her, no not falling.

Dripping.

Pools of silver liquid surrounded her, brushing off of her skin like water. Flickers of flames coming off of her hands.

Her eyes blazed bright blue as she glared at my father.

What the hell is happening?

Chapter 21

Andy's POV

My blood boiled as I watched Michael throw Verity against the wall. Logan and Alexi were both struggling to get free, with no success.

The heat intensified, burning me from the inside out until I felt that familiar tingle on my fingers and knew it had worked.

I silently thanked Alexi for the private training sessions, before focusing on that one spark until it spread up my arm. The chains fell to the floor, as I stood up.

Michael turned to me, a look of anger on his face.

"What the hell do you think you are..." his eyes went wide as he stared at my hands. Fear seeping into his features, as he just stared at me.

"What are you?" he whispered.

Embers flickered across my hands, slowly as my strength started to come back to me, they grew. From sparks to embers, until flames covered my arms.

Michael was yelling, he sounded distant over the

pounding of my heart.

The wolfsbane still in my system, kept me weak. It took all my strength to keep the flames lit. They flickered, growing weaker.

Michael grinned, aware of my struggle.

Taking pleasure in it.

Wolves flooded into the room, growling and snarling. All of them staying back, eyeing the flames from a safe distance.

"Did you truly think you could win? I will not let you survive this time little wolf."

Ignoring the arrogant alpha, I braced myself for the attacking wolves.

Planking my feet firmly just in time as the largest wolf lunged for my throat.

My hands reached out, instinctively. The wolf wailed, falling to the ground. The reek of singed flesh filled the room, as the wolf whined. Chunks of his skin blackened with blisters.

Michaels voice boomed, drawing our attention.

"Hurry up and kill her, you useless fools."

The wolves bowed to their alpha, before turning back to me.

Logan struggled against his chains, uselessly. Alexi joining him, trying to help, to do anything but just sit and watch. The burning heat on my arms lessened, weakening.

I can't keep this up for much longer, I need a plan.

Anything.

Another wolf lunged for me, knocking me back. Using all my strength I heaved the massive wolf off of me.

Applying the last of flicker of flame, I have to the wolfs skin, causing a cloud of smoke to surround him as he was engulfed in flames.

The heat on my hands lessened until they were back to normal.

The final two wolves snarled, readying themselves for an attack.

They both lunged for me, the first knocked down easily, the second however collided with me.

Bothe of us falling to the ground. A howl left my lips as the wolf's teeth latched onto my leg.

"Andy." Logan's voice echoed through the room, his anger seething into it.

The wolf bit down again and I could feel the muscle tearing.

Come on, get up.

He goes for my leg again, his jaw opening. Teeth barred, blood dripping menacingly on the floor.

"Let her go." Someone growled, silencing everyone in the room.

It can't be...

Connor stood at the door, teeth showing as he glared at the wolf above me.

"This is not your fight, boy."

"We had an agreement." Connor hissed.

Michael huffed, ignoring the anger in his words.

"You never told me who *she* was."

Connor growled at Michael, inching closer to me.

Logan visible stiffened as Connor got closer.

How can he be here?

"Enough of this nonsense, kill her." Michael ordered.

The wolf above me turned its head towards me, but before he could attack, he went flying across the room.

"Now." Connor yelled.

Within seconds the whole room erupted in chaos.

Grayson and Derrick rushed through the door, heading straight for Michael.

Tackling him to the ground.

Connor came towards me, helping me to my feet.

"What the hell are you doing here Connor?"

"Saving your life, you're welcome."

"You expect me to thank you? I've been kidnapped twice and both times you were involved."

Connor shrugged; an apologetic look on his face.

What the hell is going on.

"Perhaps we can have this discussion later..." Grayson commented, as he broke Logan's chains.

Nodding, I ran towards my mate, Logan wrapped his arms around me.

"Are you okay little one?"

"A bit bruised but I'll live, how about you handsome?" a smile covered his face.

"I'm okay. You had me worried, we really need to stop doing this."

I agreed and we walked towards Alexi. Damon was undoing his chains, as soon as he was freed Alexi ran towards Verity.

"Are you hurt? Love, are you okay? I'm so sorry."

Verity stayed silent, unable to get a word in as Alexi nervously rambled.

"Let the poor girl speak Lex." Logan said, smiling. Alexi shifted on his feet, running his hands through his hair. Verity smiled reassuringly at him before turning to look at me.

"I am sorry, for my father."

I hugged my arms around her.

"You have nothing to apologise for."

I released her, Alexi instantly wrapping an arm protectively around her.

"I do believe I missed something." Logan said, laughing at my confused expression.

"When did you find your mate?" he asked Alexi.

Crap.

Alexi looked at me confused before answering.

"When we arrived, did Andy not tell you?"

Logan's eyes darted to mine.

"You knew?"

"Yeah, so it may have slipped my mind." I admitted.

Logan shook his head.

"What distracted you? Nothing else important has happened since we have been here?"

Verity looked at me, her eyes wide. They still didn't know, and in a creepy torture dungeon is not where I pictured telling my mate I'm pregnant.

Before I could defend myself, Grayson came running up to us.

"We have a problem." He said as he reached us.

"What is it?" Logan asked.

"I can't reach the pack." Logan stiffened, and I knew why.

We were all here, the alpha, Luna beta and gamma. Blue Moon was weakened because of us.

We need to get home.

Logan rushed to Connor, grabbing him by the throat.

"What did you do?"

Connor struggled against his brother, trying in vain to break free.

"I didn't do anything, this wasn't me."

"Sure, it wasn't." Logan growled.

"I just wanted to escape; I didn't want any of this."

"It doesn't matter what you wanted; chaos follows you. I swear, if anyone gets hurt, brother or not I will kill you myself." He growled out before dropping him to the ground and walking out the room.

"Who is he?" I heard Verity whisper to Alexi.

"No one important." I said before following my mate.

Connor winced at my words, unable to look me in the eye.

Logan was pacing in the hallway; I could feel his stress.

As soon as he saw me, he pulled me towards him. Burying his face in my neck, breathing in my sent he started to calm down.

"I'm sorry little one."

"It's fine handsome, I would've don't it if you hadn't."

Logan smiled at me, keeping one arm wrapped around my shoulder.

"We need a plan."

Logan nodded his agreement.

"I can't shift, I doubt any of us can. There's too much wolfsbane in our systems."

"We will have to drive back; Grayson and the others can run though and get there first."

"Sounds like alpha to me."

We walked back to the room, Alexi was trying to calm Verity and another girl.

"Where is he? What did you do?" Verity was shouting, as Alexi held her back.

Michael was on his knees, chained. A smirk covering his face.

"What's going on?" my words came out quieter than I had intended.

"My mate, Sam. He's not here. Michael sent him out this morning."

"The beta?" Logan asked her.

She nodded.

"What did you do?"

"What's right." Michael replied.

Everyone started to speak, Logan growled silencing

the room.

"Grayson, Damon you go back to the pack. We are still full of wolfsbane so we will take a car and follow you."

"Yes Alpha, what about him?" Grayson asked, motioning to Michael.

"He will come with us; he will answer for what he has done."

Again, Grayson nodded, and he and Damon hurried out the door.

Damon paused, unsure if he should continue. He shook himself before following Grayson.

"Grab you things, we leave in fifteen minutes." I said to Alexi before walking towards the door, Logan following behind.

Chapter 22

Verity's POV

Andy and her mate left the room, leaving us in silence.

Molly was terrified, shaking nervously, her eyes never leaving Michael.

Alexi's arm was wrapped around my shoulder protectively. As if it were the most natural thing. A small smile played on my lips; I have a mate.

Michael is in chains.

He can't hurt Alexi anymore.

I have a mate. The words repeated in my head.

"You okay love? We need to get our things and head out."

We.

I looked up at him, stunned. It hadn't even occurred to me that they may have meant me as well.

Alexi started to look worried, shifting on his feet.

I can leave Silvercrest.

"Okay, my rooms upstairs."

Alexi's face brightened with the biggest smile.

Molly smiled too, watching us. Her smile however didn't reach her eyes.

"I'm going to miss you V." she whispered.

My heart broke for my friend, she was going to be left alone with her monster of a mate.

An idea cam to me and I turned to my mate.

"Do you know where Andy went?"

Alexi nodded, before motioning to the last remaining Blue Moon warrior to watch Michael.

"Follow me."

Alexi led the way out of the dungeons and upstairs until we reached one of the visitor suites.

I turned to Molly, smiling reassuringly.

"Stay with Alexi, I'll be right back."

Alexi let me go alone, reluctantly.

Knocking on the door, I heard Andy say.

"Come in."

Andy stood by the bed, a warm smile on her face.

"Is there something you needed Verity?"

"I need to ask both of you something."

Logan stopped packing clothes away and came to join us. They both stood, patiently waiting for me to speak.

"Well, I wanted to ask a favour. You've done so much for me already, and I'm sorry to ask."

Andy chuckled. "Just ask Verity, I'm sure we can help."

"My friend Molly, you met her before. She's Sam's mate."

Andy nodded.

"She's my only friend here, and when we leave, she will be alone with him."

"You want to know if she can join us?" Andy asked.

I nodded.

Andy looked at her mate for a brief second before answering.

"It would be our pleasure."

Before I could stop myself, I wrapped my arms around Andy.

"Thank you, so much."

"You're welcome, if you both hurry we can all head back."

Nodding I ran out the door grabbing molly's hand and pulling her in for a hug.

"They said yes."

Molly looked at me confused.

"Yes, to what?"

"You can come with us."

Molly stopped and stared at me shocked.

"We can both be free Molly."

Her senses came back, and she hugged me tightly.

"Go pack quickly, meet us outside."

Molly nodded and ran towards her room.

"We have to get packed too love."

I led Alexi back to my room, it was on the other side of the packhouse. Next to the kitchen, they had converted the old storage room for me, with an ensuite bathroom so I had no reason to mix with the other pack members. Alexi stood at my door, staring at the small room.

"This is where you sleep?"

"Its not much, but at least this one has a bathroom. The last one was worse." He growled, stopping me in my tracks.

"Sorry love, I didn't mean to scare you. You deserved better than this." He reached out, brushing his fingers across my cheek.

"I'll help you pack."

"No need, I'm done." I said, holding up my backpack.

"That's all your bringing?"

Shuffling, I told him the truth.

"That's all I have."

He pulled me towards him, wrapping two strong arms around me.

"After all this mess, we will have to fix that."

Ten minutes later we stood outside the packhouse. Me, molly and Andy were all waiting for the cars. After a few seconds in silence, Alexi and Logan pulled up. I had given Alexi the keys to my father's cars, the warrior had already taken one with my father secured in the back.

Logan was driving his car, Andy in the passenger seat. Alexi opened the door for me to get in the other car with him, molly climbed in the back.

Alexi drove, following closely behind logan and Andy. His hands gripping the steering wheel anxiously.

Driving must feel slow to a wolf, being stuck in a car not being able to shift and run full speed to the fight.

He's a beta, his packs in trouble and there's nothing he can do but hope he makes it in time.

My hand reached out instinctively, wrapping my fingers around his arm.

Sparks travelled across my fingertips as Alexi relaxed under my touch.

His grip loosened, one of his hands reaching over to grab mine.

The ride was agonisingly long, we reached the pack as the sun was beginning to set.

The sound of pained howling filled the air. Logan's car turned sharply, heading away from eh pack. Away from the howling.

"What is he doing?"

Alexi followed him.

"I'm not sure, there's nothing out this way. Well, nothing except..."

Alexi cursed.

"The arena, they're going to the training arena."

"Why?" Molly asked.

"Weapons, its filled with them."

A few seconds later a massive brown bricked building shielded by trees came in to view.

We all shuffled out of the cars, Logan and Alexi ran inside the building.

They emerged holding a mass of metal, swords, shields even what looked like an axe.

We all took a weapon, me and molly choosing small daggers.

"Have you two had any training?" Logan asked us.

We both shook our heads.

"Only men were allowed to train, we learnt to cook."

"Arsehole." Andy muttered.

Alexi turned to us.

"Stay close to me, keep the knives with you just in case.

We both nodded and then we all shuffled back into the cars, heading towards the danger.

Chapter 23

Alexi's POV

Chaos, that's the only way to describe the packhouse. Warriors surrounded the building, blocking the exits as rogues tried to fight their way in.

Andy dint hesitate, sword in hand she ran to the nearest attacking wolves.

The mood changed instantly, and the warriors realised their Luna and Alpha were back, fighting with them.

A sandy blonde wolf caught my eye, as soon as she saw me, she ran straight for me.

Placing her muzzle in my hand, whimpering slightly.

I felt Verity tense behind me, moving closer to me.

The wolf eyed her curiously, before her eyes went wide.

Smiling a big wolfy grin as she stared at Verity.

"We are in the middle of a rogue attack."

The wolf raised an eyebrow at me, well the wolf

equivalent anyway.

I could almost hear her saying.

"Shush, there's always time for introductions." Shaking my head, I obliged.

"Verity meet my mother, mother this is Verity."

Verity stiffened again, nervous. She stayed mostly hidden behind me.

"Hello." She whispered.

My mother nudged Verity, still smiling. Verity relaxed, smiling back.

Howling drew all our attention, my mother went to run back to the fight.

"Mother, wait." She stopped and looked at me confused.

"Can you protect them?" I said, motioning to Verity and Molly.

She nodded, coming to stand beside the girls.

I turned to Verity, running my fingers across her cheek.

"Stay with her, she will keep you safe."

The girls both nodded, as I turned and ran towards the fight. Ignoring the urge to stay with my mate, to protect her.

The rogues were all attacking Logan and Andy, they seemed hell bent on killing Andy.

A large muddy brown wolf led the rogues, keeping them trained on Andy.

"Nice of you to join us." Andy yelled as I reached them, never taking her eyes off the attacking wolves.

Rolling my eyes at my sister, I grabbed the nearest wolf by the throat.

Holding him back as his teeth bit the air, trying to get Andy. She turned, stared at the wolf before bringing her sword down onto the wolfs neck.

"Why are they going so crazy? It's like they're feral." Andy yelled.

She was right, all the wolfs looked wild. Their eyes clouded over, fur knotted. It wouldn't have surprised me if they started foaming at the mouth.

But one wolf stood out, the leader. His eyes were clear and focused, fur clean and he seemed to be ordering the other wolfs.

What the hell is happening.

Laughing drew all our attention, standing in front of the pack house stood Michael.

One of our warriors, Danny at his knees, face bruised and beaten.

"It's fascinating, isn't it?"

Confused we all stared at him.

"Licantile, I, I believe they call it. A gift from the hunters. Any wolf injected with the drug becomes blood thirsty, feral. Genius really. Inject a wolf and he will take down his entire pack."

Trying desperately to get through the wall of feral wolves, to get to Michael. Watching as he lifted Danny up by his throat, needle in hand.

"Here, I'll show you." He said as he plunged the needle into Danny's neck.

His eyes went wide, his bones involuntarily snapping as he confused. Falling to the ground in a whimpering heap. After a few seconds he went quiet. Shifting painfully into his wolf, eyes clouded, growling ferociously at the others.

"Amazing, turns out they can follow orders, provided they are simply enough. For instance, kill the Luna."

Danny took one look at Andy and started growling, before lunging for her. The wolves had all surrounded Andy blocking us from her.

Andy kept fight, knocking wolf after wolf away.

Danny reached her biting at her arm. Yelping Andy pulled her arm back, tearing the flesh on Danny's teeth.

"Andrea." Logan yelled, still trying to get through the wolves.

I watched Andy, she was on the defensive. Avoiding attacking Danny, only defending herself. Trying desperately not to fight him, even though he was trying to rip her apart.

She's, his Luna. My wolf spoke up.

The wolfsbane must be wearing off.

Obviously...

Idiot, a Luna protects her pack, it is against her nature to harm one of her wolves.

She doesn't have a choice, if she doesn't defend herself, he'll kill her.

Agreed.

"You have to fight back." I screamed at my sister. Ignoring the snarls of the wolves around me.

"Leave her alone." Verity's voice echoed across the field.

Michael glared at her before showing his teeth in a menacing smile.

"You're right girl, I should fulfil my promise. After all you have ignored my warning again.

Verity paled, fear flooding her features.

For a second, I thought he was going to attack her.

I was wrong.

Simultaneously all the wolves turned and leaped for me.

Knocking me to the ground, the muddy brown wolf snarled. His paws holding me down as his jaw collided with my shoulder.

"Alexi." Verity's voice echoed through my head as the world went black.

Chapter 24

Verity's POV

I watched in horror as Sam lunged for Alexi, biting down on his neck.

Alexis mother howled, her face torn. She wanted to protect her son, but she didn't want to leave us alone.

Powerless I watched my mate go limp, blood covering the ground around him.

Sniffling came from behind me, and I knew Molly was crying.

"He can't. I won't let him." She whispered before walking towards the fight, ignoring our protests.

I'm sorry. She linked before turning to face Sam.

"Stop."

Toms large wolf turned to her, snarling. For a second, I thought he was going to attack her, but he just snarled and went back towards Alexi.

"You won't hurt him, I won't let you."

They both stared at each other, a private

conversation happening as we all watched before Molly straightened herself and spoke with such confidence, I felt proud for my friend.

"I Molly Tanner reject you Samuel Lloyd as my mate."

Silence.

Every wolf was silent as Sam howled, hunching over in pain. Clawing at the dirt beneath him as the mate bond broke.

Tears fell from Molly's eyes as she watched him whimper in pain.

Every wolf around Tom paused, unsure of how to proceed. Using their distraction Andy ran to Alexi, kneeling beside him.

Ignoring the protesting wolf in front of me I ran to my mate. One phrase repeating in my head like a prayer.

Please be okay.

My pulse sped up as I reached his still form. Blood surrounded him, dying the grass a dark red. A chill went down my spine as my stomach dropped. lifeless and pale Alexi wasn't moving, Andy was trying to stop the bleeding, yelling for help.

I know Im surrounded by battling warriors, but I don't see them. All I see is Alexi, all my focus on his pale face.

This can't be how it ends.

Shakily I knelt beside him, gripping his hand in mine. His skin felt like ice against mine, the sparks so weak I could barely feel them.

Alexi reacted to my touch, a moan slipping from his lips.

"Verity?"

"I'm here, stay with me."

He tried to smile, but was too weak for it to reach his eyes.

His grip tightened on my hand, the slightest pressure as he held on to me.

"I'm so sorry, please stay with me."

My voice cracked as tears fell freely down my face.

"Not your fault." He whispered.

"Yes, it is, if you had never met me, none of this would be happening."

His hand reached out to me, as he tried to wipe the tears from my cheek. Moaning slightly as the movement caused him pain.

"I should have been stronger, I tried to stay away. I

tried to keep you safe, I'm so sorry." My voice became barely audible as I sobbed beside him.

I felt movement as someone knelt beside him, a woman leant over him. A growl slipped from my lips, and she turned to me. Her red hair framing her face as she smiled at me.

"My name is Dr Hope, I'm here to help sweetie." Her voice remained calm as she stared at me, her hands remaining on Alexi, eager to attend to her patient.

My ability to form words was still in question so I simply nodded, and she got straight to work. Tearing the remaining scraps of his shirt and throwing them aside.

"His healing is slow."

She didn't phrase it like a question however Andy answered her.

"He's got wolfsbane in his system."

The doctor nodded and went back to her examination. Her focus completely on her her patient, completely ignoring the chaos around her.

I held my breath as I watched her try to stop the bleeding without much success. Her brow furrowed and her eyes went wide.

"Luna, I need your help."

Andy was instantly at her side.

"What can I do." She asked, eager to help her brother.

"Burn him." Andy paled and the doctor continued.

"If I was in surgery, I would cauterize the wound, but I do not have the equipment here."

Andy's voice shook and for the first time since I have met her, I saw fear in her eyes.

"We can take him inside."

"We can't move him, he won't make the trip."

Andy's face fell.

"Tell me what to do." She whispered. Doctor hope reached for Andy's hand guiding it to Alexi's shoulder.

"Only light your finger, if you do you whole hand it will kill him."

Andy stilled, her eyes impossibly wide.

"No, no I can't. I've never done that before, there has to be another way." She begged. The doctor look at her apologetically.

"I'm sorry dear, we don't have time for this."

Andy closed her eyes taking a deep breath she put

her hand on Alexi's shoulder.

The pressure caused him to moan.

"Please Lex, you can't move. I'm so sorry, but you cant move."

Even weak he still tried his best to smile at Andy before going motionless, holding his breath to avoid moving.

Andy whispered another apology as she closed her eyes again.

After a few painfully slow seconds her eyes opened. A bright blue shine, moving like flames. If it was a different time, if my mate wasn't lying on the ground close to death, the sight would have mesmerised me.

Alexi's screams pulled me from my thoughts. So much pain in that one sound, how could someone survive this.

The smell of burning meat overwhelmed me as Andy tried to calm him.

"Please Lex, please stop moving."

Alexi ignored her, still thrashing in pain. The doctor grabbed his legs holding him down.

"Verity, grab him. If he keeps moving, I'll kill him."

I caught his head in my hand, the other on his good

shoulder holding him in my grip.

His eyes flew open, and he howled with more strength than I would have thought he had left.

Putting my face directly in front of his, making sure he could see me.

"Alexi please, listen to me. Stay still, as still as you can. I know it hurts and I'm sorry, but you can't move."

Again, he groaned, trying to get away from the pain.

"You are not aloud to die, do you hear me? I just found you, I wasted so much time trying to run. Scared because of how I felt, scared because I was falling in love with you. You are not aloud to give up."

Alexi stilled his teeth clenched together with the effort of it.

After an agonising, few seconds Andy whispered.

"Done, I...I think it's done."

Dr Hope moved to examine her work. We all waited, none of us daring to breathe until she spoke.

"The bleeding has stopped."

Alexi sighed, his muscles relaxing.

"You're not out of the woods, we need to get you inside."

Alexi nodded, bracing himself for the movement he knew would come.

Logan appeared it of nowhere, lifting Alexi off the ground as gently as he could.

"Heard you needed a lift." Logan said, trying to keep his voice light. Alexi smiled up at him before his eyes closed again.

Logan carried him away from the packhouse, towards a large blue building.

We walked through the sterile hallways, the smell of bleach and cleanliness overwhelming my senses.

"Last room on the left Alpha, I will get scrubbed in, the nurses will take care of him."

Logan nodded to the doctor as she walked away, before taking Alexi through the big metallic doors.

"Alpha." Two nurses, gowned and ready greeted Logan, motioning to the bed in the centre of the room.

Once Alexi was laid across the bed they got straight to work. First cleaning the wound then dropping a cloth over him.

Once they were satisfied, they pulled a tall machine towards him, covering his face with a mask.

"I'm sorry alpha, you cannot be in here for surgery."

Logan nodded turning to leave he stopped as he passed me. His eyes softened and he reached out to take my hand.

"We have to let them work Verity."

I couldn't look away from Alexi, lying unconscious, still covered in blood.

"I understand how you're feeling, please we have to go."

As I looked into his eyes, i saw the honesty in his words.

"How did it end? For you I mean."

Logan smiled." you can ask her if you like."

Andy.

"Was she as bad?"

He looked away before answering.

"Worse."

"How did you survive it?"

His smile returned.

"Alexi."

After a slight pause he ushered me out of the building.

"Come, let's check on Andy and your friend."

Nodding, I let him lead me outside and across to the packhouse.

We both stopped as we took in the sight of them.

Andy stood in the centre of the field, the grass around her blackened. Molly stood in the door to the packhouse, her eyes wide, staring at Andy's back.

Andy turned her eyes blazing a fiery blue, when her eyes met Logan's, they instantly calmed.

Walking to us she wrapped her arms around her mate.

"What did we miss?" Logan asked.

Chapter 25

Andy's POV

Logan carried Alexi, with Verity following closely behind. Damon's voice pulled my attention.

We could use some help.

I watched my mate carry my injured brother wishing I could follow, but Damon was right. They needed help.

Forcing myself to leave my brother I went back to the fight.

Damon and a few other warriors crowded in front of the packhouse, all keeping a barrier between the house and the attacking wolves.

Distract Danny, keep him away from here. I ordered Damon.

His wolf looked at me, his eyes connecting with mine. He shook his head.

Just trust me.

Again, the wolf shook his head.

I needed him to listen we were already down Logan

and Alexi. So, I used the one thing I knew would work.

Listen to me, the guy smiling over there, he's the reason the hunters attacked my pack. He sent them.

The wolf started growling, ready to lunge for Michael.

I need you to get Danny away from here. Please.

You want me to let him go?

This time it was my turn to shake my head.

I want to stop them all, but I can't risk hurting Danny.

His eyes locked with mine again before he nodded.

Damon ran, biting at Danny as he passed. Danny instantly responded, chasing Damon away from the fight.

"This is my pack, leave it now or you will not get the chance again."

His smile grew wider as he glared at me.

"Cant you see, you've already lost." He said, as if it were completely obvious.

"Your forgetting something." I replied, same obvious tone in my voice.

His glare intensified, threatening to burn through me.

"And what's that?" he asked, trying to keep his voice the same calm tone, but failing miserably.

"Wolfsbane only last so long."

My lips turned up in a smile as I linked the warriors around me.

Run

Without a second of hesitation, they all ran for the packhouse. Taking cover. Maybe understanding what I had planned, or perhaps the blazing colour of my eyes made them run. Regardless, they were safe inside.

My eyes went back to Michaels as my hands heated up. The wolves all turned to me, instantly lunging toward me.

They didn't make it far before the flames reached them, singing their skin. The smell of burnt me surrounding me.

Michaels smile faded, still glaring at me as the wolves tried and failed to reach me.

The heat kept growing, spreading around me until a circle of flames engulfed me. Taking every wolf with it. Those that still had some sense howled and ran.

Pained howls came from around me, as the wolves struggled and tried to break free. When the howls had past, and silence fell the flames died down as the air around me cleared.

Michael was still glaring, rooted to his position. His hands fisted at his side as he watched his makeshift army of rogues fail.

Even for an alpha, he was stubborn. Any normal wolf would have accepted they lost and be running. Its our instinct, we fight for those we love, but we also give up to protect them too.

"You have lost, there's no chance for you now. Surrender." I yelled, a part of me hoping he wouldn't. after what he did to Alexi, a big part of me wants to make him feel the pain Alexi felt. And to feel the pain he's put Verity through, to have to grow up with that man.

The growling in my head made it obvious my wolf agreed. For everything he has done, to my pack, to his, to Alexi to logan to me. He deserves every ounce of agony I can give him.

"I haven't lost, you think I will run like those pathetic boys." He motioned to the woods beside us, where the wolves had run.

"You believe me to be that weak? I am an Alpha." He roared, lunging towards me.

Shifting into a massive bronze wolf inches before

he reached me.

No matter how much my wolf wanted to fight, to show her power, neither one of us was going to risk our pup.

So instead, I ignored my instincts keeping my arms up blocking him, I held my feet as his wolf tried to connect with my face.

Using my feet, I shuffled out of the way just enough to make him lose his balance knocking him to the ground.

He growled at me, moving to get up. Before he regained his footing I lunged for him, my fists coming in contact with his neck as we fell to the ground. He howled in pain as I grabbed his arm twisting it, until a crack echoed in the open air.

His eyes darkened as he glared at me, still trying to escape my grip.

Shifting our positions I grabbed his throat, wrapping my arm around him. I felt him tense before reaching around, grabbing hold of my shoulders and hurled me over his head. With a crash my body collided with the ground, Michael inching closer to me, teeth showing as he snarled at me. Lunging he pinned me to the ground, I felt the heat slowly spread up my arms again. To slow.

The wolf smiled menacingly at me, his claws impaling my shoulders.

Suddenly I felt the wolfs weight withdraw from me, his claws slashing my shoulders as they were pulled out.

A few feet from my head, Damon had his mouth around Michaels leg. Twisting at a horrible angle.

Michael howled in pain, clawing his way out of Damon's grip. Michaels claws sliced through Damon's side, With a whimper Damon released his hold.

Before Michael could attack again, I used my whole body to collide with him, knocking him to the ground. My fists collided with his face, bone crushing under my fingers.

He did this to me.

He made me an orphan.

Still my fists kept going, ignoring everything else but the anger that had built up.

Every ounce of pain in my life could be traced back to this man. Everyone I mourned, every time Connor and his friends beat me.

All of it.

Logan's face crossed my mind.

My handsome perfect mate, my parents and Alexi. My anger dissipated as I looked at Michaels bloody face.

Standing up I grabbed Michael by the scruff of his neck, he struggled as I dragged him.

Damon stood, still shifted, eyeing me curiously as I threw Michael at his feet.

"I'm not the only one he put through hell. He's all yours."

The massive wolf bowed his head to me, the first sign of respect he's ever shown me, before lunging at Michael.

Turning, I headed towards the packhouse, injured wolves surrounded the house both theirs and ours.

The sound of footsteps had me turning, ready to fight what ever wolf decided to come back.

Logan and Verity both stood staring, Logan with an impressed smirk and Verity staring at her friend who had come outside of the packhouse.

Running to Logan I wrapped my arms around him, the anger I felt instantly disappeared.

"What did we miss?"

"Nothing much, just dealing with a pest problem." Logan chuckled, his eyes settling on the blackened grass.

"We may need a new lawn." I shrugged.

His chuckle turned in to a full on laughing fit as he

pulled me closer to him.

"I do love you little one, you never cease to amaze me."

By the time his laughter had died down, I must have had the biggest, stupidest grin on my face.

The packhouse doors opened as the warriors all came out, shifted back in their human forms they searched the bodies. Trying to find anyone who may need help. We all went to join them, searching for any signs of life.

"How is he?" I asked as we went through the wounded.

Logan looked at me, his eyes glistening with unshed tears. My breath caught as I stared at my mate. Panic filled me and Logan ran to me, wrapping his arm around me.

"He's okay, he's in surgery. I didn't mean to scare you, Andrea. I'm so sorry."

My heart rate calmed as I stood in my mates arms. My eyes fell over a still honey brown wolf and I froze. Running to him I knelt beside him and checked his wounds.

"Who is it?" Logan yelled.

"Grayson." I whispered, in a split-second Logan was by my side.

Grayson laid, so still, lifeless. I was sure he wasn't breathing, but as Logan's hand touched the gash on his head. Grayson whimpered. Without another word, Logan bent down and lifted the massive wolf. Carrying him towards the hospital.

A nurse rushed straight out with a gurney, motioning towards Logan.

Once they were satisfied that Grayson was in place they rushed inside, leaving us all waiting outside.

"Come on, let's check on Alexi." Logan whispered, grabbing my hand and pulling me inside. Verity close behind, staying extremely quiet.

Chapter 26

Verity's POV

Chaos, so many wolves were wounded, their bodies laying scattered across the lawn. Warriors were attending to every wolf as quickly as they could. Molly smiled at me, the emotion not reaching her eyes before she headed inside.

It didn't bother me, my friend had been through a lot today and I knew her well enough to know she needed some time.

Logan rushed to Andy, the movement was so quick it drew my attention.

The two of them were lent over an injured wolf Logan lifted him and we all walked back towards the hospital. The closer we got the more anxious I was to see Alexi, to know he was okay.

I spent so much time, worried about what could happen that I never considered the alternative. That maybe I would get my mate. That I would get to experience anything close to what I can see in Andy and Logan. The way his eyes gravitate to her automatically. The way they shift closer together, so that they are always within reach of each other. Just watching them makes me yearn for my mate, to see him, to feel him. To have him close to me.

"Verity?" Andy whispers, walking towards me.

Looking at her I realise we have made it to the hospital, Logan's no longer holding the injured wolf and is staring at me, a worried expression on his face.

I force a smile on my face before I say, "I'm okay."

She looks unconvinced but doesn't stress the issue further. Instead, she wraps an arm around my shoulder like it's the most natural thing and leads me towards the hospital. I don't think I'm ever going to get use to this, to the feeling of... it takes me a minute to think of a word that fits. Acceptance.

Alexi's scent washes over me and everything else fades away apart from him. Andy must understand because she doesn't stop me when I pull away and follow the scent. It leads me to a closed door with a number four nailed into it. My hand goes straight to the door handle, not reaching it before it rattles, and the door opens. I come face to face with doctor Hope, she jumps slightly as she notices me there. But her face softens, and a smile crosses her lips, and she looks at me.

"Hello dear, I didn't see you there."

I smile back, my eyes trying to see around her. She notices my struggle and moves to the side, motioning for me to come inside. Without hesitating I rush past her, straight to the hospital bed.

To Alexi.

He looked so pale, lying there covered in bandages. The room smelled like bleach, the same as the rest of the hospital but I tried to ignore that even as it singed my nose.

He's alive.

That one thought kept running through my head as I ran towards him. Stopping an inch from the bed.

"He's going to be fine, he will be here over night. But his wolf has already started to heal again. You may stay with him if you would like, just make sure he gets some rest. I'll have someone bring in a few blankets for you." The doctor said before leaving the room. Andy and Logan both came in, Andy reaching over to kiss her brother on the cheek before they left. Saying a quick goodbye.

Sitting on the chair beside his bed I curled up and waited for my mate to wake up.

It wasn't until I felt someone wrap a blanket around me that I realised I had fallen asleep. It took me a few seconds before the sparks along my arm registered and I opened my eyes.

Alexi was leaning over me, tucking a blanket

around me. His eyes met mine and he smiled.

"Hello Love."

I stood straight up trying to usher him back to bed, but he wasn't having any of it.

"You're supposed to be in bed, the doctor said you needed to rest."

He raised his eyebrow at me smirking.

"I don't know why you're smiling, get back to bed." His smirk only grew as he made a show of bowing to me.

"Yes Ma'am."

I knew my cheeks were heating up, but I ignored them as I helped him get back into bed.

After a few seconds of silence as Alexi watched me pace the room he asked. "Are you okay Love? They didn't get near you, did they?" I shook my head and he relaxed under the blanket.

"Logan stayed with me after you got hurt."

"Then what's wrong Love? Somethings bothering you."

"It's my fault." I whispered.

Alexi made a move like he was going to get up again, but I rushed to him, pushing him back down.

"This was not your fault Love."

"Yes, it was, if I had stayed away, you wouldn't be here." I yelled, gesturing to the room around us.

"You didn't put me here, *he* did." Alexi growled out.

I turned back to him to see his eyes had darkened to a pitch black.

"Because of *me*." I whispered.

He went to stand again, my expression stopped him, and he held out his hand. "If you don't want me to get up, can you come here Love?"

As soon as I was within reach of the bed he pulled me to him, wrapping his arms around me as he rested my head on his chest. For awhile we just sat there as his fingers brushed through my hair until he spoke up.

"None of this was your fault, I promise Love. You didn't do anything wrong."

"I was never supposed to even get a mate. And when I met you, I tried to stay away, I really did."

Alexi stilled, his eyes staring at me with so much emotion I had to look away. To look at anything else.

"What do you mean, not supposed to have a mate?"

Staring at my hands, I could feel his eyes on me. Taking a deep breath, I spoke. It all coming out in a rush as I forced the words out.

"I don't have a wolf, without a wolf I could never have a mate. I was born too early, I'm a runt. That's why my father hated me, because I'm weak."

Alexi's grip on me tightened as he buried his head in my neck, calming himself before he spoke.

"You are not weak, you stood up to your Alpha."

Alexi held my face between his hands, forcing me to look at him. "That's not weak. Wolf or not you are my mate Verity."

I blinked away tears, refusing to let them fall. Not while my mate is holding onto me. My mate. Those words repeated in my head. He's mine. A smile spread across my lips and Alexi relaxed. A smile playing at his lips as he looked at me.

"There is one question I do have Love." His smile only grew as I nodded my head.

"Well, more of a statement really, so if I remember you correctly. I do believe you said or rather yelled you were falling in love with me."

Chapter 27

Alexi's POV

"Well, more of a statement really, so if I remember you correctly. I do believe you said or rather yelled you were falling in love with me."

I watched blush cover her cheeks as her eyes went wide and she looked away.

Making sure I looked extra hurt I whispered, "Unless of course you were lying, so you wouldn't have to feel bad if I died." Her eyes went impossibly wider, and her mouth dropped open. Before she all but screamed.

"No, no, I swear."

I smiled at her. "So, you do love me?"

Again, her face froze in shock until she recovered, grabbing a pillow and hitting me with it.

"You tricked me, that is so not fair."

She kept hitting me until I faked an injury and she stop instantly checking my bandages. When her eyes landed on my face again, I couldn't keep the smirk off it. Her eyes narrowed and she went back for the pillow.

"You are so awful." She screamed.

I grabbed the pillow before it could touch me.

"You know you *love* it." I said, making sure to emphasise the 'love'.

Groaning she threw her hands in the air, cussing under her breath.

"What am I supposed to do with you?"

"I can think of a few things." I smirked.

Her face heated up instantly as she looked away.

Reaching out for her arm, I pulled her towards me. Wrapping my arms around her. She curled up on my chest. The sound of her breathing slowed until eventually she was sound asleep.

My eyes started to feel heavier, but I kept fighting them, enjoying the sensation of having my mate asleep in my arms.

Eventually I drifted into a peaceful sleep as exhaustion took me.

Chapter 28

Andy's POV

Logan led me outside, his hand around mine in a death grip.

"Where are we going?"

Ignoring my question, he kept leading me into the dark woods. Away from the packhouse. Eventually he stopped, turned to me and whispered.

"Close your eyes."

Raising my eyebrow at him I shook my head.

"You remember what happened the last time you said that, right?"

He smiled at me, but something about it was off.

Something about him was off.

He was hunched over, shuffling on his feet. His hands continuously running through his hair.

My strong confident mate was nervous. Something about that had my stomach doing flips.

Sighing I closed my eyes, still keeping his hand in

mine, refusing to let go of him.

After a few more steps he whispered in my ear, ticking the back of my neck.

"You can look now."

My eyes flew open to see the most beautiful thing I have ever seen. Trees along the path were all lit by white lanterns dangling from the branches, swaying slightly in the wind. All leading to a break in the trees with a small table, a bouquet of roses and a box of chocolates in the centre.

"What do you think?" Logan asked from behind me, his voice unsteady.

A smile on my face I turned to my mate. Gasping as I saw him.

He was on one knee with a little purple velvet box in his hand. The small silver moon ring glistening in the moonlight. The diamond sat in the centre, two crescents hugging it on either side.

Logan's eyes watched me as I stood there frozen.

"Andrea, you are the strongest and most amazing person I have ever met. I fell for you before we were ever mates and each day I fall more and more. Will you marry me?"

Tears fall from my eyes as he talked.

It was only when he cleared his throat that I

realised I hadn't answered him.

"Yes, always yes." A smile spread over his face as he slipped the ring on my finger. His lips came crashing down on mine as he pulled me closer.

When we disconnected both of us had to catch our breath.

Logan wrapped an arm around me, pulling me towards the table. I stopped walking and Logan paused, turning to stare at me. Eyebrow raised, as he searched my face worriedly. I know I must look as nervous as he did, if not more.

"What is it, little one? What's wrong?"

I smiled at him, intertwining my fingers with his.

"Nothings wrong." I whispered.

I watched him relax slightly as he waited for me to continue. Taking a deep breath to calm my racing heart I whispered.

"I'm pregnant."

His eyes widened as he looked at me, in a blink of an eye he lunged for me, wrapping his arms around my waist swinging me around. Giggling like crazy as he kept spinning me.

His paced slowed until he was just holding me, my feet dangling off the ground. His arms wrapped lightly around my stomach.

"We're having a pup." He roared.

"Shush, if we tell anyone before our mothers, they will kill us."

Logan's face paled.

"Very true." He whispered, shivering uncomfortably at the thought.

Placing me on my feet he rushed me to the table. I mean rushed, I had to jog to keep up.

"Why are we running?"

He smirked at me, leaning down to whisper in my ear.

A shiver ran down my spine as his breath tickled my neck.

"The sooner we eat, the sooner I can get you upstairs and we can celebrate properly." He winked at me.

He actually winked.

Suddenly I'm not hungry, for food anyway.

Grabbing the chocolates, I turn around. He eyes me up confused.

"Dinner in bed?" I ask, still walking towards the packhouse.

Logan growled, running after me, lifting me up.

"Lets see if we can make twins." He said before rushing us in the packhouse.

Chapter 29

Verity's POV

Alexi only stayed in the hospital for a day before they released him. We went back to the packhouse, Alexi happily showing me around all the rooms before we finished the tour in the kitchen.

Andy was decorating cupcakes with another woman I don't recognise, Logan was sitting down chatting to another man I didn't know. They all paused looking up at us as we walked in.

Andy smiled, coming over. Wrapping her arms around us.

"Welcome home." She said before moving aside as the two strangers came over pulling Alexi in for a hug.

"You children truly are going to be the death of us. First your sister now you. No more surprises, okay. My heart just can't take anymore."

Logan chocked on his drink making Andy giggle.

Within a heartbeat all eyes were on me.

Moving closer to Alexi, I smiled at everyone. The

woman, who I'm assuming is Alexi and Andy's mother raises her eyebrow at Alexi, arms crossed.

Sighing he moves aside, motioning to them he says.

"Verity, these are my parents. Mum, dad this is Verity."

They both smile warmly at me before rushing over, embracing me in a hug, trapping me between the two of them.

When they released me, I knew I was grinning like an idiot.

"Welcome to the family dear."

Thanking them a giggle left my lips as I watched Andy shove a whole cupcake in her mouth. Frosting covering her lips as she winked at me.

Mrs Jackson looked at her daughter.

"Really Andrea, you couldn't just eat it, rather than inhale it."

Andy just stared at her mother, reaching for another cupcake. Staring intently at her as she very slowly shoved the thing in her mouth. Whole. Again.

Shaking her head in disapproval, a smile tugged at the corner of Mrs Jacksons lips.

Andy puts her hands up, waving them in mock

surrender.

"Fine I'm stopping."

A gasp comes from beside me as her mother all but yells.

"What is on your hand?"

Andy puts her hands down shrugging again.

"Nothing."

"Andrea Hale, show me you hand."

Sighing, Andy reaches her hand out, showing a beautiful ring.

Her mother squeals before pulling her in for a hug.

"Alexi open the champagne, we're celebrating."

Alexi nods reaching for a bottle, pouring glasses for his parents, Logan and me.

When he got to Andy, me Andy and Logan all said no at once.

Logan looked at me, tilting his head before looking back at Andy who just shrugs.

"Have I missed something?" Alexi asks, staring at the three of us.

Another squeal sounds from her mother as she looks between us.

Sighing Andy just nodded, Logan smiling beside her, his eyes shining with pride.

Her mother rushes to her.

"Goddess, I can't believe it."

"Seriously have I missed something?" Alexi whines.

I couldn't stop the laugh from leaving my lips, his eyes narrowed at me. Which only made me laugh harder.

Everyone joined in, laughing as Alexi crossed his arms. Glaring at all of us.

Eventually I caved, he looked so frustrated I had to put him out of his misery.

"She's pregnant, you idiot."

Alexi's eyes widened as they flew to Andy.

"I'm going to be an uncle?"

Andy just nodded as Alexi rushed to her. Lifting her up swinging her around.

They were both giggling like children as they stopped spinning. Andy grabs another cupcake, shrugging at all of us.

"I'm eating for two, shut up"

Her mother laughed.

"When weren't you eating for two my dear."

Everyone started laughing as Andy stuck out her tongue at us.

"I've got to start planning an engagement party, baby shower and wedding." Her mother exclaimed excitedly.

Andy's face paled causing us all to laugh again.

After the celebration Alexi led me upstairs, into a massive bedroom. His scent washed over me, and I knew it was his room. The walls were covered in bookcases lined with piles of books, CDs and DVD's. everything from terry Pratchett to the diehard movies. One wall was bare apart from a painting of the night sky right in the centre.

"What do you think?" Alexi asked, his voice quieter than usual.

"We can change anything you want, it's yours too after all."

That had me turning, he was standing next to the bed watching my reaction.

"It's perfect." His face lit up and he wrapped his arms around me, pulling me towards him.

"I'm glad you like it Love." He whispered, as he buried his head in my neck. His breath tickled my neck, and a shiver ran down my spine. His lips brushed my ear and sparks shot through me, leaning into his touch I felt his chest shake as he chuckled.

His finger pressed under my chin, lifting my face to meet his. Our eyes connected and I watched as his eyes shifted to my lips.

He lent towards me, stopping just before our lips touched, unsure of himself. Something in me pushed me forward, my lips crashing down on his. He tensed for a second before leaning into the kiss.

This wasn't anything like our first kiss. Nothings stopping me from accepting my mate now. No Alpha, no fears, no insecurities. Alexi knows everything about me, and he still wants me.

And I want him.

I want all of this.

Leaning into the kiss I felt it deepen as my hands found their way in his hair. Tugging it slightly.

A growl slipped from his lips as his hands slipped to my hips. He pulled me closer, pressing my body against his. I felt my feet leave the floor as he lifted me, my back softly hits his bed. Alexi never breaking the kiss. A moan leaves my lips causing Alexi to growl in approval.

Our lips disconnect and his eye find mine. The pale

blue almost glowing in the dim light of the room.

"Are you sure?" he whispered, eyes still fixed on mine.

"I promise Love, I can wait. I will always wait for you."

My heart flutters at his words. Running my fingers along his cheek, smiling as he leans into my touch. Taking a deep breath, I respond sounding a lot more confident than I felt.

"You don't have to. I know I haven't made it easy, but I promise that was only ever because of my father, I always wanted you." His smile grew impossibly wide as he tried to respond but I put my finger to his lips, silencing him.

"And, I say this of my own free will. Not because you're hurt or dying or because I don't want the guilt. I love you Alexi Jackson." His eyes widen and his lips come crashing down on mine. Melting into the kiss my hands find their way to his hair, again tugging him closer.

Suddenly he pulls away, causing a whimper to leave my lips.

What the hells happened to me?

A smirk covers his face as he leans down, kissing me again, softly.

"I'm not going anywhere Love, nothing in the world could drag me away from you in this moment."

Smiling I try to pull him back down, but he wouldn't budge.

"I just need to say one thing. You amaze me."

He looked at my confused expression and continued.

"You survived so much and you're still kind. You're fearless, I know you don't believe it, but you are. You stood up to Michael to protect me and Andy. You are amazing, kind and beautiful Verity, and I love you too."

As soon as he finished, his lips come crashing down on mine again. His hands roam my body, one landing behind my head pulling me closer, the other stroking up my stomach, pulling my shirt up.

Sparks explode through me, like my own personal firework show as he touches me. Moaning my hands copy his, caressing his stomach to his chest.

I moan softly as I unbutton his shirt, I quickly take it off with his help. His mouth moves from mine trailing kisses down my neck over my breasts, squeezing them slightly.

A moan leaves my lips, and he smirks up at me. Lifting my shirt off before his mouth descends on my breast. His tongue rolling one nipple as his hand roams the other. My moans grow louder as his free hand travels down. Pulling my jeans and moving my panties aside as he teases my clit.

"Alexi" I all but beg as he teases me, my body craving release.

The bed shifts as he climbs off, causing me to glare at him.

A sexy smirk covers his face as he takes off his jeans and boxers, leaving him naked.

My eyes travel down almost instinctively until I reach his member. A gasp leaves my lips.

That is not going to fit in me. His smirk grows before he climbs on me, our lips locking again.

I feel him pull my jeans off completely, throwing them across the room.

His eyes darken as they roam my body.

"Are you sure?" he whispers, his eyes connecting with mine.

"Completely." I whisper.

He smiles down at me, as he positions himself. His eyes never leaving mine. Once his member touches my opening, I take a deep breath as he presses into me, impossibly slow, allowing me to get use to the feeling. The pain only lasts a second before it vanishes, replaced by ecstasy. Shifting my hips, I push against Alexi's slow thrusts.

Noticing the shift in me Alexi starts to push harder, speeding up.

The feeling in my stomach is amazing and crippling, I feel as if I could die a blissful death at any moment. The fast thrusting from Alexi was almost too much, my body unable to keep up.

"Alexi." I whimper as the pleasure takes over me, begging for release.

Alexi shifts, his mouth going to my neck as I feel his teeth grace my shoulder questioningly.

"Yes." I almost scream out.

His canines sink into my shoulder, my body quivers and releases the pleasure inside of me.

I moan loudly as does Alexi before I feel him harden and twitch inside of me.

We both collapse on the bed, trying to catch our breath. A moment goes by, and he pulls me towards him, my head resting on his chest.

"I could get use to this." I whisper causing him to chuckle. His arms tighten around me, and he pulls me impossibly closer.

I look up at this man and a feeling of home fills me, instantly warming my heart. This beautiful man is my home.

And his next four words have me completely and utterly addicted to him.

"Ready for round two?"

To be continued in book 3…

Chapter One

Megan's POV

"I can't believe you actually agreed to go, this is amazing." Wes beamed at me; his smile so big it showed his teeth.

"It's not like I'm going because I want to, what else could I say."

Wes rolled his eyes at me.

"Exactly, the Luna personally invited you, how cool is that."

Shaking my head, I give up. I can't win this argument. To Wes going to some pack party is the most exciting thing to ever happen.

There was absolutely no way to convince him otherwise. Shuffling through my wardrobe, trying in vain to find shoes to match the Luna's dress.

"This is useless, I have nothing to match it."

"Oh, hell no, you are not getting out of this. You

finally agreed to go."

Wes stood his ground, hand on his hips. Eyebrows raised as he waited for me to argue.

There really is no point.

Enjoy yourself, we deserve some fun. My wolf purred.

We have always been so different I sometimes wonder how we can possibly be one.

It's just a party...

Well then it should be easy...

Wes stood up and ran out of the door.

Moments later he rushes back in, bright silver heels in his hand. Raising a brow at him, he just shrugged.

"Stole them from Annie, she won't even notice. Now hurry up and get dressed."

Rolling my eyes, I do as he says. Smirking as I turn to him.

"I forgot to mention, I have a plus one."

His eyes widen, mouth drops open and he growls

at me.

"And you waited until now to tell me? Oh, my goddess, I have nothing to wear." raising my eyebrow, my hands fell to my hips as I wait for him to stop freaking out.

"We both know you have something to wear."

He huffs at me.

"Nothing new, I can't go to the Alpha and Luna's engagement party in old clothes." I rolled my eyes again before turning to the mirror applying makeup as he huffs behind me.

"It's a masquerade, no one's going to know it's you."

"I'll know." He grumbled before storming out of the room.

Ignoring him I turned back to the mirror.

The dress was beautiful, and hugged every curve I had. The baby blue fabric made my caramel skin pop. Even my brown eyes looked brighter.

I silently thanked the Luna for sending it to me. Her note replaying in my head, making me smile.

Megan,

Saw this and thought of you. Please come to this ball, I need back up!

Love Andy x

Ps: a plus one is totally approved, I'm going to need an army.

Thirty minutes later and Wea was running back in the room, in a perfectly fitting blur tux. A blue mask covering his face, his short brown hair slicked back.

"Nothing to wear?" I teased as he rolled his eyes at me. Bowing slightly, he reached out an arm to me.

"My lady?"

Giggling I took his hand and we walked outside. Getting in his truck before driving to the pack house.

They had out done themselves. Lanterns lined the drive up to the house, all the way to the ballroom.

The ballroom was lit with the most beautiful tealights, covering the walls. Everything about it looked right out of a fairy-tale. Eyes landed on me and Wes as we walked in, making me eternally grateful for the mask covering my face.

"I can't believe we're here." Wes whisper/yelled in my ear. I couldn't help but smile at my friend, he was so excited.

The Luna and alpha were both on the far side of the room to us, laughing with the beta and his mate.

Andy looked stunning, her purple ballgown flowed around her as she walked, seemingly weightless.

Wes clutched my hand, pulling me towards the dance floor.

"What are you doing? You know I can't dance." I whined as he pulls me to him. His arm wrapping around my waist.

We was always a good dancer, me on the other hand was awful. After few minutes of me clumsily tripping over my feet and Wes laughing at me, I finally gave up.

Untangling myself from him, he chuckled again,

pulling me closer. I stared at him confused but he just smirked at me before lifting me up and placing me on his feet.

"I'm not five." I whined.

"Maybe, but you dance like a five-year-old."

I stuck my tongue out at him, which only made him laugh harder.

We stayed on the dance floor for what felt like hours before the smell of orange and pine trees brushed over me, making me freeze.

"You, okay?" Wes whispered.

No, please be wrong.

My wolf started howling in my head and I knew exactly what her next words were going to be.

Mate! She yipped excitedly.

I felt eyes on my back, as footsteps approached me.

Wes was staring at me, worry covering his features. He pulled me closer to him as the footsteps got closer.

A growl sounded behind me, sending a shiver down

my spine. Wes bowed his head, his wolf submitting to him.

The stranger went to grab my hand, Wes reluctantly released me, stepping back. His eyes glued to mine the whole time.

Sorry. He whispered through the link.

I gave him a small smile, not trusting my voice, mental or otherwise.

The stranger took my hand, sparks erupted on my skin as he turned me around.

Not a stranger, our MATE. My wolf growled at me.

He is a stranger, do you know his name?

She huffed but stayed silent.

His hand went to my waist as he swayed, holding me against him.

I could feel his eyes burning holes in my skin, but I couldn't bring myself to look at him.

After a few seconds of silence, he reached out, putting his finger under my chin. Lifting my head forcing me to look at him.

My eyes connected with his beautiful grey ones,

the rest of the world faded away as we stared at each other.

His face was half covered in a black mask but what I could see was gorgeous. From his black hair slicked back from his face to his strong jawline. He was at least a foot taller than me, in a black tux.

But those eyes...

They're mesmerising, almost like a thunderstorm. Endlessly powerful, getting lost in them would be way too easy.

His hand goes to his face, and he removes his mask. My breath hitches in my throat as his face comes into full vicw.

It can't be.

He smiles at me as he reaches out to my face. My senses come back as his fingers graze my face, going to take my mask off.

Without thinking I turn and run.

Ignoring my wolves howls or the growling coming from behind me.

He can't be my mate.

Grayson O'Connor cannot be my mate.

ABOUT THE AUTHOR

Alexa Phoenix writes funny, action-packed, steamy paranormal romance. Her characters are clever, fearless, and adventurous but in real life, Alexa spends all of her time curled up with a book in her hands, daydreaming. Let's face it. Alexa wouldn't last five minutes in one of her books.

All are welcome to join my book club on Facebook, Alexa's Book Club, to keep up with new releases, promotions and freebies.

As always, reviews and comments are not just welcome but encouraged.

Facebook: AlexaPhoenixFantasyWriter

Tiktok: alexaphoenix23

Instagram: alexaphoenix23

Patreon: Alexaphoenix

Linktree: linktr.ee/alexa_phoenix

BOOKS BY THIS AUTHOR

Rejecting the Alpha

Life has a funny habit of throwing the most peculiar curveballs at you.
Up until now I thought my life was fairly ordinary, but I was so wrong.
After losing my parents two years ago, I found it hard to believe in anything.
Then I met him... Oscar Campbell.
He has changed my entire perspective on life and the world around me. The supernatural world exists and it's closer than any of us realize.
Oscar has awakened something inside of me that I didn't know was there.
I just don't know if I'm ready for this new life.

Mated

I thought I could hide forever, but fate had other plans.

I can't remember what it feels like to be happy. I'm sure I felt it long ago, back when I thought I was in love. Great husband, great job, great life. Great big lie. At least, that is what my life has turned into now – a series of lies to hide the fact that I am not who I appear to be. The lies keep me hidden and safe... for now.

Surely, my ex-husband would never think to look for me in this sleepy little town. As I settle into my new life, I'm afraid it won't be forever. Could I really give up my job and best friend to go back on the run? Then, I meet Hunter and my world flips upside down.

One night of passion is all I can offer, but he wants more. That's the last thing I need, yet I find myself craving what I can't have. I can't deny this intense attraction that keeps pulling us together like a magnet, and he's not going to take no for an answer.

My heart fills with hope, but it only takes a moment for it to shatter. I'm not the only one keeping secrets, and Hunters are even bigger than my own.

A single mistake is all it takes for me to put his life at risk, and sooner or later my web of lies is going to catch up to me.

With everything spiraling out of control, I can only be sure of one thing... my life will never be the same.

Made in United States
Orlando, FL
12 October 2023